THE LAST ORACLE OF LAZIROTH

THE SHADOWLAND SAGA
A NOVELLA
2.5

STEPHANIE ANNE

Cover design by Celin Graphics
Book Formatting by Derek Murphy @Creativindie
ISBN: 978-0-6455011-0-0 (paperback)
ISBN: 978-0-6455011-0-0 (e-book)
FIRST EDITION: JANUARY 2023

FOR LOVERS OF DRAGONS, DESTINY, AND BRANDON THORNE.

FOR ANYONE FIGHTING.

FOR MY UNCLE, JOHN, WHO FIGHTS EVERY DAY

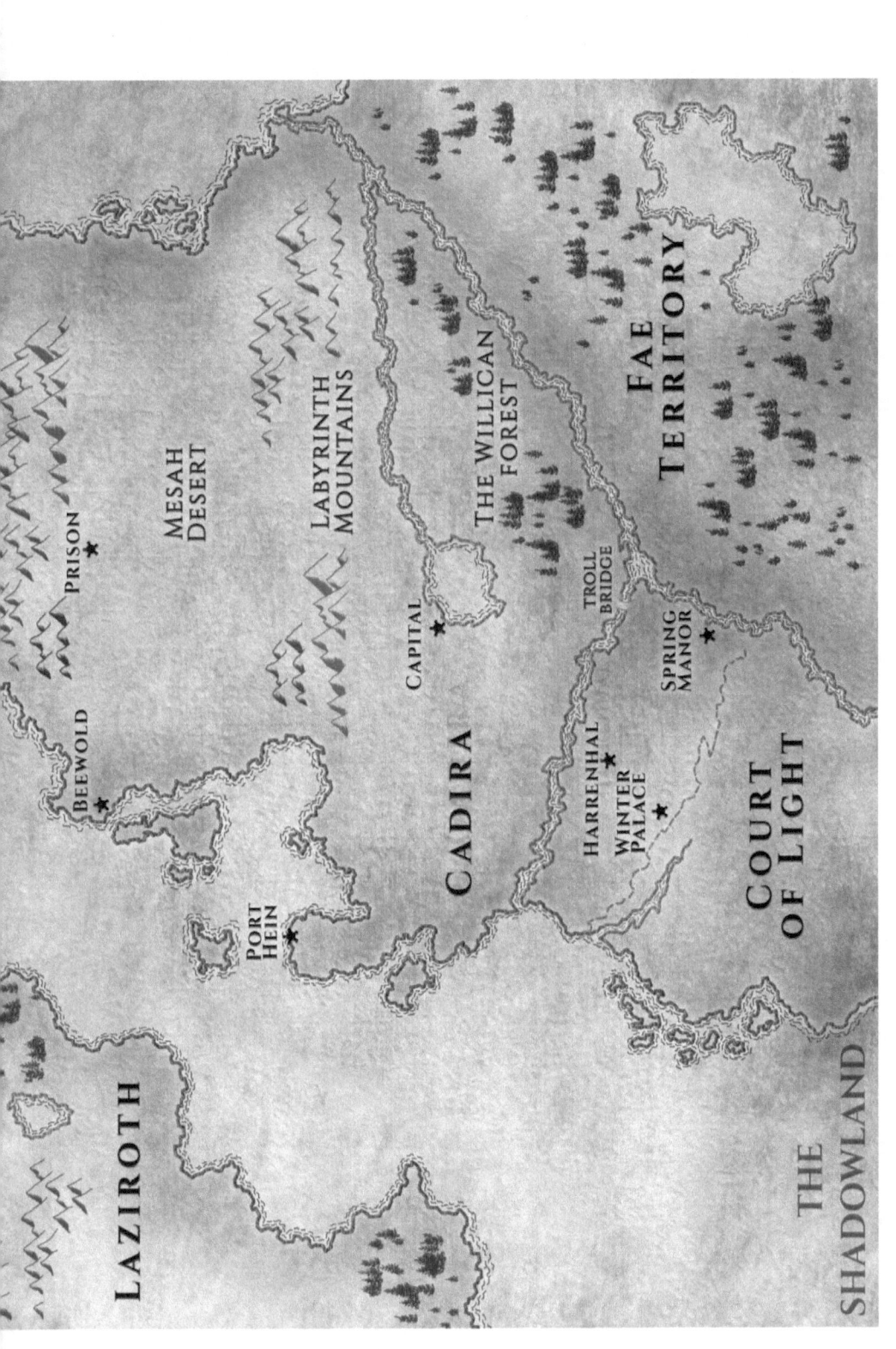

1

THE LAND ACROSS THE SEA

Brandon Thorne rode into Port Hein before the sun could crest the horizon and blanket the land in soft pinks and oranges. Each thundering step that took him further away from the capital and Eliza made his resolve slip away. He knew that in order to save her, he had to leave. Isolde's voice echoed in the back of his head, her warnings and her fears replaying in his ears. So with her blessing he continued on, forcing himself not to look back.

It didn't stop the guilt growing in the pit of his stomach, did not quench the unyielding fear that he had made a mistake in leaving the palace. That by doing so caused irreversible damage to his relationship with Eliza.

But the ball was only a reminder of what he couldn't save her from, that he could not protect her from the will of the Blood Witches, or the commands of the king.

Descending the hills that led into the port city, Brandon pushed thoughts of Eliza and her birthday ball aside. Instead, he focused on what he knew: the dagger was lost, forgotten to even the oldest of beings. He could not travel the unseen landscapes of the Fae Territory, but the continent west of Cadira was just as old and steeped in an ancient magic that predated Cadira, with stories so old they were written in tongues unteachable now.

It was in Laziroth he had last found answers, a purpose. He hoped they would grant him the same favour again.

Entering the port-side city reminded him of Eliza, of their journey north into the desert. That day should have changed everything; he should have turned around, returned Eliza to the king, and continued the quest on his own. Perhaps he could have saved her all the pain that came with Mesah and the tunnels that ran beneath the sand.

But he hadn't, and for that he would hate himself forever.

Brandon shook his head and dismounted at the edge of the city. His steed, a chocolate brown mare, threw its head and made a soft whinnying sound.

"It's alright," Brandon murmured, rubbing a hand down the mare's neck. "You will be fine."

He found a garrison of soldiers on the outer edges of the city, only a small troop of around twenty or thirty guards. Their only purpose in Port Hein was to oversee the shipment of goods, but Brandon had spent enough time in the Cadiran Military to know they had more to do than met the eye.

The soldiers asked no questions and gladly took his horse to keep in their stables. The garrison looked worn, tired. But Brandon couldn't ignore the change in the air, the way the people talked about their lost prince being found, how he was soon to be married to the witch who saved him. Their spirits were already brighter compared to his time spent with soldiers like them at the Winter Palace.

Brandon left the garrison with his head lowered. He clenched his jaw. The truth of Alicsar ate at him, and since the prince's return to Cadira, hearing the people gush over how perfect he was, more than infuriated the commander. Because he knew deep down the prince was nothing more than a façade, that beneath the vulnerability was a darkness that had once threatened Eliza's life.

And Brandon needed to know if that darkness would rear its head once more.

During the weeks that followed Prince Alicsar's rescue and the truth of his amnesia, Brandon had seen the difference between him and Dorin, the alter-ego he'd assumed while on Eliza's journey north. Late night discussions with Celia almost had him believing Dorin and Alicsar were two different people.

But he could see the way the knowledge warred inside Eliza. She couldn't separate the two egos. Deep down, Brandon hoped she wouldn't, that the two wouldn't change in her eyes.

Dammit Thorne. He clenched his fists and turned sharply into a dark alley, secluded from the prying eyes of the military and the townspeople. Before he could think better, he slammed his fist into the brick wall opposite him.

"Dammit," he hissed, shaking his hand out. He knew better. Or at least, he should have.

But whenever Eliza was involved, he wasn't sure what he should do next.

Brandon looked towards the hills that marked the land between him and the capital. It would be so simple, he thought, to return, to apologise for not being at the ball. He could just go back and finish helping her like he had promised.

But Isolde's voice whispered in the back of his mind, with warnings he couldn't ignore.

He closed his eyes and leaned back against the brick wall. He needed answers, some sort of guide through the ever changing terrain of his world. The oracle of Laziroth would give him that, at least.

If a war was coming—and he was sure it was—then he needed to be certain they were ready.

Brandon shoved his hands into the pocket of his cloak and ducked out of the alley with his shoulders hunched and head lowered. The docks were alive with fishermen and crews preparing to go out for another day of sweeping the sea floor for fresh fish and lobsters to grace the king's table. Carts with ice boxes designed to withstand the trek to the palace were already pulling to a stop at the docks, prepared for another long, winter day of hauling stock to the capital.

Brandon passed the crews, searching for a dock master. Men checking nets and baskets along the old, rotting wood dock didn't look up as he passed. Women made their way out of the warmth of their homesteads to help send the men on their way. Brandon lifted his head; a stout man with a silver moustache and a brown, leather hat glared at an open book, his narrowed eyes glancing between names messily scrawled and the boats anchored in front of him. He stood several paces from the docked ships and wore the hat despite the overcast day. His clothes weren't neatly mended like the dock master's in the capital, but scruffy and worn, dulled by the sun and age.

When Brandon approached, the dock master paused and looked him over once. Ruddy cheeks pinched as he frowned. "What do you want?" he asked, pursing his cracked lips

"Passage," Brandon replied, careful to keep his voice low, "to Laziroth."

The dock master snorted. "Aye, good luck with 'at."

Brandon clenched his jaw; he slipped a hand into his pocket and pulled out a grey pouch heavy with silver coins. They clanged as he dropped it onto the open pages of the book, where the names of the different ships were scrawled across the parchment with their merchandise and port fees.

"I'll pay."

The dock master glanced between the pouch and Brandon. After a moment of silence, the older man shrugged. "End of the harbour. Laziroth trading vessel. Might take you 'cross."

Brandon said nothing as he shoved his hands into his pockets. He kept his head bowed as he passed fishing crews preparing to set sail.

If he were lucky, he'd be able to leave in a matter of hours. It would take several good days at sea, but he'd arrive in Laziroth by the end of the week, and depending on which port the ship docked in, if he had a horse it would take him little time to arrive at the final town before the mountainous hike to the oracle.

Had there been more planning involved in his decision, perhaps he could have booked a ship across to set him in his final destination, but he hadn't even thought his plan through. Amitel's reappearance, their failure at protecting Alastor and Xeb, and Eliza's marriage forced him to decide: stay in Cadira where he might find nothing of the dagger, or leave for a land where the old magic still existed, and the oracle remained trapped in her temple?

A black figure caught his eye, flashing across his vision.

Brandon stopped, not far from the old fountain that had once been a portal into the forgotten tunnels of Azula's cities.

The figure ducked down an alley; Brandon recognised it as the one Eliza had led them down when they'd first arrived in Port Hein, the alley where they'd overheard the demon talking to its master. It should have been the moment he'd sent Eliza back to her world, where she would have been protected from the Dark Master.

Brandon tensed, his hand sliding to the pommel of his sword. If Shadow Soldiers had followed him to the port...

He didn't want to think about what might happen if the Dark Master found the oracle, what it might mean for Eliza.

Brandon swept his gaze over the dark walls, down the wet cement, to the dead end where he expected to see the figure. But the ally was empty, save for him.

He tasted no magic in the air; the hairs on his arms weren't raised from the electricity of a portal opening and closing. If one had appeared at the end, he was sure he would have seen it.

Eyes narrowed, Brandon stepped into the alley.

Pain exploded in the back of his head, and before he could take another step, the world around him went black.

2

BEFORE

Smoke clogged Brandon's nose as he and Amitel slipped through the darkness that blanketed the edges of the sleepy riverside village. Above the river, where the village was dense, a deep burgundy highlighted the silhouettes of houses and a great cathedral sitting against the outline of the mountains. The fire had yet to reach the turrets, but it steadily climbed towards the peaks that broke through the water surrounding it.

Amitel swore under his breath as they traced the snaking road down to the river's edge. "Surely they didn't have that much of a start," he said, breaking through the tree line first to take in the destruction wrought by the mercenaries.

Brandon descended slower and stopped behind the warlock. Within the trees he could have perhaps forced himself to believe the fire wasn't ruthless, that the burgundy creeping along the horizon was the fault of the rising sun, waking up the sleepy water village.

But breaking through the line of trees, he knew better.

It engulfed the western side of Varun, thrashing within the water. People screamed for help that wouldn't come, rushing to boats already spread far throughout the river, bobbing away from the destruction and fire threatening to encompass them.

"They're going to wipe everything out." Brandon's heart squeezed in his chest. He'd seen destruction like it before, during the war; the smoke clogging his nose no longer smelt like still river water and instead burnt like pine, and rather than houses on stilts, he saw stone cottages turning black with soot.

Brandon blinked, and the white faces of people fleeing during the sun's highest point disappeared. Instead, the tired, scared faces of Lazirothian people spilled out around him. The old woman who had offered them board in her small house on the edges of the village, the fisherman who had brought them across from the other side of the river, children who had played in the shallows catching crawfish. Women weeping for stolen husbands, men standing at the edge of the river, watching as their homes burned.

Brandon swallowed thickly. "Enya, her men... they're going to destroy everything so no one can follow them."

"The oracle is still in the village," Amitel said, cutting down to the road. There were people stumbling from their houses, running to the water's edge, where their boats should have been moored at the thin dock.

But Enya and her crew must have cut the ties of all the boats, so no one could help—or escape.

Amitel seemed to have thought the same as he stopped by a family cursing in Lazirothian, their faces dark with tears. The golden-haired warlock looked back at Brandon; his eyes, usually a burning gold, were a bloody red, glowing in the night. Wind swept his hair back from his face.

Brandon couldn't move from the shadows; he felt the heat of the fire warming his brow and yet he couldn't blink away the pine forests of eastern Cadira, where creatures born of darkness and shadows had appeared from the ocean to take the northern mountains.

When he blinked, the shadows disappeared and Amitel was no longer near the family; he'd stalked to the edge of the dock and raised his hands, palms down to the water. He said something, and slowly the waves crept towards the dock, rocking the boats closer to the shore. The magic spilled like vines from his fingertips, striking the water like lightning, gripping the small waves and forcing them closer, bigger.

Several of the men rushed forward; with arms outstretched, they reached for a nearby boat, a smaller vessel, used maybe by two or three people to get to the river village. Brandon cursed himself and descended into the village, making his way to the men.

Dropping down beside them, Brandon reached for the edge of the boat. It brushed against his fingers, then rocked away.

He released a frustrated breath and turned to Amitel. "Could you bring it closer, please?"

The warlock's red eyes found his. "I am doing what I can. The magic is... strange here."

Brandon frowned, but he said nothing more as Amitel lifted his hands higher and moved them in a rocking motion that brought the boat into the dock.

Before it could crash into the rotting wood, Brandon clenched his jaw and took hold of it, steadying it within arm's reach. When Amitel dropped his hands, Brandon and the other men dragged it into the dock.

"What will you do?" one of the men asked, voice dark with fear.

"What can we do?" another said.

Brandon rose as Amitel met him by the boat. "We'll try to ferry as many over as we can," the warlock said, climbing into the boat. "Be prepared to take in anyone escaping the fire."

"One little boat cannot help," a woman replied from the shadows of safety. "There are hundreds needing passage."

Brandon climbed into the boat with Amitel and picked up an oar. He spied a larger vessel and nodded towards it. "We'll row to that one, take it to the village. Someone over there should be able to ferry it."

Amitel looked between him and the boat; it had trawler nets hanging off either side, though thankfully they hadn't been lowered into the water. But it was large and could potentially carry twenty or so people.

Another man approached them. "That is my boat," he said, eyes on the trawler. "Please. Let me come with you. I will help. It is not easy to navigate."

Brandon and Amitel shared a look. "Alright," Brandon said after a moment. "Climb in."

The small boat rocked, not intended for three larger men, but it didn't tip. The threads of Amitel's magic steadied it long enough for Brandon and the other man to start rowing; the water felt like sludge to pull through, and although he'd hoped they weren't too far behind Enya, the results of their failure floated past them, bobbing in the dark waters.

The smell of wet wood burning couldn't drown out the stench of burning flesh.

At the edge of the trawler, Amitel steadied them long enough for the man to climb the side first, taking a loose rope in his weathered hands and using the side of the trawler as an anchor to climb. The man threw down the rope and Brandon caught it with ease, climbing up the side of the hull. At the top, he knelt and offered the warlock a hand.

"Does this mean you officially like me, knight?" Amitel asked, waving away his hand and instead took the rope.

Brandon pressed his lips into a thin line and shook his head. "Not a chance, warlock."

He stepped back as Amitel climbed aboard; from the back of the boat, a loud *clank* caught his attention. Sparing the warlock a quick glance, Brandon rushed back to find the man they'd travelled with on his knees beside the device used for steering.

"It is broken," he murmured, staring at the ruined pieces. "They destroyed it."

The same tendrils of magic Brandon had witnessed earlier crawled towards the device; before his eyes, the splintered wood mended.

Brandon looked back to find Amitel lowering his hand. "There. And it will sail without wind or force. Just think and we will move. It'll work so long as there are people needing passage."

The man blinked and nodded. "Thank you. Thank you."

"Just get us to the docks." Amitel turned and walked to the front.

As the vessel jolted, Brandon followed the warlock, keeping his eyes on the raging fire. "Is there anything you can do to stop that?"

"Not without completely starving the fire of air, which may result in hurting more people. And if I use the river against it, I risk drowning anyone nearby and killing them."

Brandon stopped and crossed his arms. "It's a simple fire. I've seen Blood Witches take out more."

Amitel whirled. "It is a living flame. It feeds off of life." The warlock scrubbed a hand through his shoulder length hair. "So long as there are souls for it to take, it will breathe."

The fire leapt and crackled, and as they neared, the sounds of screams grew louder. There were people attempting to reach the water; some were so desperate they attempted to swim, but the water steamed with the heat of the living flame. With each swing of their arms, they cried out in pain, their skin raw from the heat.

Brandon rushed to the side and threw the rope into the water. A woman, no older than thirty, with a child clinging helplessly to her neck reached for the end, crying and spitting water. With a grunt, Brandon hauled her aboard, clenching his jaw. The strength of the Brotherhood made it easier, but it still surprised him just how strong he was.

Amitel was at his side a moment later, pulling the woman aboard and tending to her burns, soft golden light radiating from his long fingers and palms.

Brandon threw the rope again and aimed for another person, but their hand slipped beneath the water as their head did, and they did not come back up.

From the back of the vessel, the captain shouted, and they slowed as they reached the dock. A convergence of people rushed to the side, as more appeared from a dark alley, escaping a pair of sword wielding mercenaries. Brandon threw himself off the side of the boat and rolled onto the dock, barely missing the scrambling victims as he rose and released his sword from its sheath. The mercenaries stopped as he appeared in front of the crowd, and with cries of their own, they rushed him.

Amitel called his name, but Brandon succumbed to the calm of the fight; in his head, he could hear the Brotherhood's trainers as they taught him how to focus the magic in his blood into his strength and speed, the mindset a warrior—a *knight*—of his station would need in order to win every fight, every battle.

Deep in the back of his mind, he heard *her*, laughing as he fell into Lake Mab, where not even the Blood Witches dared swim, or the soft whisper of her voice as she called his name in the early mornings before the war.

He let the cool whisper of her breath against his ear, the grazing touch of her fingertips, calm him as he swung the stolen blade into the approaching mercenaries. He recognised the pair that met his blades; both were of Lazirothian descent, with similar almond shaped dark eyes and hooded brows, stubble lining the strong angles of their jaws. They had twin scars on their cheeks, like claw marks from a beast, that glowed pink under the red light of the fire.

Brandon tightened his hand around the hilt of his sword and ducked an attack from the twin-sword wielding mercenary, swiping across the gut of the second who appeared on Brandon's other side. The second dropped with a grunt, blades falling from gloved fists to clutch at his wound, while Brandon returned his focus to the first.

The mercenary glanced down at his fallen friend, then met Brandon's eye with a glare. He said something in one of the many languages that spread across the large continent, then pushed forward with a shout. His swords swung in a flurry of silver, glinting orange and red in the night. Brandon met every strike; each blow made his teeth rattle, but he dug into the well of strength the Blood Witches granted him and pushed on without falling, without succumbing to the darkness that had been clouding his mind since he left the front lines north-east of the Labyrinth mountains.

Brandon palmed a small dagger and flipped it once before burying it into the first mercenary's side, pushing it up into his ribcage, into the man's lung.

He dropped beside his friend.

The dagger fell from his grip, clattering to the docks. Brandon curled his fingers over the hilt of his sword. He punctured each man's heart, ending their lives without remorse. Brandon wiped the blade clean on the cotton undershirts of the second mercenary and turned as Amitel approached. The trawler pushed away from the dock and started for the dark, northern shore. There were a few people left, stolen weapons in hand, their faces tired but stances prepared for any who might try to stop them.

The warlock looked at the two mercenaries and shook his head. "Feel better now?"

Brandon snorted and shook his head. "I'll feel better once Enya is dead, and the oracle is back in her cage."

Amitel made a face. "Easier said than done."

They started down one of the many wooden paths that crossed through the town, towards Enya's establishment. The small, sinking structure sat somewhere in the centre of the village, near the old hollow cathedral, hidden in the shadows of the tall buildings built around it, their silts hiding it from direct view.

But Brandon followed Amitel through the dark corridors between houses and taverns, where the smoke grew thinner. As they ran, they pushed people in the direction of the dock, helping some out of the water and pulling others away from the corpses of their loved ones. There was little they could do for the people, not until they found the source of the flames.

Not until they killed Enya.

The establishment, a small nook in the village, was home to a number of black market items that wouldn't normally appear in a town such as Varun. But the village was the perfect front for such things; with the old cathedral offering security and items for the taking, and the people being none the wiser, Enya had been able to create a reputable business for herself. One that threatened to destroy everything in its wake.

Brandon and Amitel stopped in the shadows of a nearby business and hid behind a pile of wooden crates; four mercenaries waited outside with crossbows and an array of weapons strapped across their bodies. They were large, brutal men born and bred for battle; had they not been mercenaries, they likely would have been picked up by the Dragon Hunters.

Amitel frowned, eyes a deep mixture of red and gold as he took in the scene before them. "The fire is disrupting my magic," he growled, tightening his hands into fists. "I can't take them out from here."

Brandon crouched and pressed a hand to the wood. Most of it was rotten, but the churning lake rocked against the panels, wetting his fingers. It was hot, warming beneath their feet. "We drown them, then."

As he rose, the warlock pressed his lips together. "One good hit would take out the dock..." He turned to Brandon. "But what about us?"

Above their heads, ropes strung between houses swung in the hot wind. Brandon reached for a hole in the wood and checked his weight before climbing. "We climb."

3

PIRATES

Brandon awoke to the taste of ash and river water on his tongue.

Stars danced across his vision as he blinked hard against the shard of light blinding him from a gap between the wooden planks above him. The taste of copper filled the back of his throat, and when he tried to swallow, he choked on his heavy tongue. His muscles ached with a familiar stiffness, the sensation common when one had been unconscious for a long amount of time.

Brandon reached up to touch the back of his head and pulled back with a hiss. Thick blood coated his fingers, his hair matted to his skull. The blood wasn't fresh, though; he'd been out for some time. It crusted in his hair and on his fingers, and the ache in the back of his skull was dull, but a reminder nonetheless.

Closing his eyes, Brandon sucked in a breath.

Idiot, he thought, releasing the breath. He should have known better, and yet...

He let his guard down.

Brandon opened his eyes; the rusted bars of the cage trapped him on three sides, the ship's hull at his back. Beyond the bars were dark crates. He moved into a sitting position, ignoring how his vision swam as he did. But as he blinked, a small hall came into focus. It led to a table and a ladder leading up. The gentle rock and the stomping of feet above told him enough—he was on a ship, and certainly not the one he'd intended on boarding.

Though he suspected he was trapped on a ship, the stench of potatoes and onions, fish and dried meat overpowered the briney scent of the ocean. The sun was hard as it beat down on the ship, warming the wood behind him and the spot in his cell.

If he had to guess, it was midday. Every couple of minutes, the sun blinked in and out of existence as someone passed overhead.

Brandon climbed to his feet and tried the bars; they looked old enough that one good shove would break them, but as he reached for the rusted metal, he felt a buzz of magic and quickly drew his hand back to his chest.

A charm. He swore, shaking his head. He knew why they kept the old cell now.

Magic trapped Brandon within the bars. If he wanted out, he'd need a key.

He'd need to wait until someone finally went down to see him.

Brandon slid to the ground, bowing his head.

He hated waiting.

~

A day passed with no answers.

Brandon paced the cell, checking the ladder and hatch every so often for any movement; his satchel and belongings sat untouched on a table beneath the ladder, forgotten. It was lucky he had two hundred years of experience that prepared him for such occasions, and yet within a day he felt useless, unworthy. It burned in his chest, whittling away at the thoughts he'd tried so hard to lock away.

He didn't sleep—not because of the head wound, which stitched itself together after several hours thanks to the Blood Magic coursing through his veins—but because he wanted to be ready for whoever finally graced him with their presence.

But as the sun passed overhead, and night fell, he became more and more aware of where he was, what was happening.

If Amitel saw him now, crouched in a cell, he would be laughing at Brandon's stupidity.

The thought of Amitel sobered him, and he closed his eyes. Brandon sucked in a sharp breath as his stomach roiled with the thought of leaving Eliza with the warlock. Perhaps he should have thought about it longer, leaving her alone with him. Amitel had given them no reason to trust him beyond claims the oracle told him he had to.

Was that enough for Brandon to forgive him?

For Eliza?

Brandon had seen what the oracle was capable of, what her knowledge could create. But if he was wrong, if it turned out Amitel was still working alongside the Dark Master...

At that thought, Brandon shook his head. Celia was still there, and he was certain she wouldn't let Amitel betray Eliza again.

A crack of thunder echoed in the hull. Brandon opened his eyes and took in the shadows that circled him.

What if the Dark Master was responsible for his capture, Brandon wondered. It was a thought he didn't want to entertain, and yet if it were true...

He sighed, shaking his head. There was no sun blinding him now; dark clouds forewarned a storm, casting his cell in shadows and turning the once warm day cold. He heard the crew above him rushing to chain down anything important. He waited for someone to secure the crates, but no one came.

If the Dark Master had him, then he had two options: find a way to kill himself so the bastard couldn't use him against Eliza, or find a way to get any and all information that might become available to him.

Both were risky. Both—

The hatch opened on silent hinges and snapped shut a moment later. Brandon stiffened as the heavy footsteps of a man climbed down into the belly of the ship. Brandon remained still, waiting with his breath stuck in his throat.

He kept his eyes ahead as a man stopped in front of the cell, dropping a stool as he did. With a groan, the man sat and smiled.

"Good," he drawled, stretching one long leg out in front of him. He tucked the other into his chest and rested an elbow on his knee.

"You're awake."

Brandon finally looked up; the man in front of him wore his long, black hair in thick locs, tied back with a thick piece of leather. His skin was a deep umber, eyes black, tinged with days spent on the sea. A dark leather vest with the insignia of a Lazirothian hunter glared at Brandon; he doubted the man in front of him was an actual hunter, but it surprised him to see the crest over the man's heart.

There was a pistol on his hip; Brandon hadn't seen many in his long years, knew that only the most wealthy and influential of Laziroth's people had them.

Brandon rested his head against the wooden planks of the ship's side. "What do you want?"

The man in front of him grinned; his teeth were yellowed, some so bad they'd fallen out. A dark beard, cut close to his chin, had beads that clanked from three long locs. They glinted silver despite the dim light.

"I am Captain Crane," he said, leaning forward, "and you... I know what you are." He paused and gave Brandon a once over. "You're one of those bastards of the Blood Witches."

Brandon blinked up at him. "What do you want?" he asked again.

Captain Crane chuckled. "To talk. Then perhaps we might come to an... agreement."

"I'm not sure what you expect of me," Brandon said, leaning forward. "But you'd be smart to let me off at the next port."

"And why would I do that?" Crane asked with a laugh, leaning back as he crossed his arms. The smell of tobacco and sweat wafted from his person with every movement, tickling Brandon's nose.

"Because I'm not who you think I am."

The captain grinned. "I think you're exactly who I think you are," he replied. "You're an immortal knight, a toy for the witches, and you also happen to be carrying around with you a military badge from Cadira."

Brandon stiffened as the captain rested a hand on his side, hovering over the hilt of a sword. It took Brandon a moment to realise that it wasn't just any sword; he would recognise the raven's head anywhere, the worn grip that had been moulded for his hand, the scabbard of his father, patched with charms and magic to preserve it. His blood boiled, and he clenched his hands into fists.

"What's a dog like you got to do with that piss-ant king of Cadira?"

For a moment, Brandon considered not answering; he pressed his lips into a thin line, keeping his eyes on the captain. Brandon couldn't read him, and that alone made his skin crawl. Was the captain a pawn of the Dark Master or an agent of his own free will?

Brandon couldn't be sure of either, but he hoped for the latter.

Crane shrugged. "Fine, don't answer." He took his hand away from the sword's hilt. "You're an interesting one, I will admit. I didn't think the Brotherhood of the Blood Witches were the type to find ships to sail to Laziroth."

"And yet, here I am," Brandon responded. "What do you want?"

Captain Crane chuckled, throwing his head back to reveal his dark neck and a scar that sliced beneath his jugular. "Immortality," he replied, leaning forward, the amusement wiped from his face. "Not the bullshit warlocks seek, no." Shaking his head, the captain rose and stalked to the other side of Brandon's cage. "I want that good stuff. The stuff only your kind can get."

Brandon followed each of the captain's movements, but he dropped his head and laughed—really laughed, despite knowing his chances of escape were dimming the longer he let the sound bubble from his lips.

He laughed at his own stupidity for getting caught by a pirate determined to live for eternity. At the worthlessness thrumming through his veins.

Brandon knew he would die at sea if he didn't stop laughing, and yet the thought didn't stop the burn of tears from lining his eyelids.

Finally, Brandon stopped and touched a hand to his eyes. "Do you really think *I* know anything about that?" he asked, dropping his hand. "Like you said, I'm a *plaything* for the Blood Witches."

The captain rose, lifting a hand to the bars. Fingers dipped in the riches of Laziroth, gold from the Empire, and glittering jewels of the Courts ran over the charms that contained Brandon.

"Perhaps another day without water and food will help you

remember what the witches did to you."

Brandon narrowed his eyes and lunged as Crane stepped away from the cell.

The captain laughed, the sound following him as he walked back to the ladder and climbed back onto the deck.

Jaw clenched, Brandon let himself fall back against the side of the ship. He closed his eyes. The lull of the ocean, the gentle push and pull of waves against the hull, carried him into the darkness of his thoughts. He let himself drown in the deep abyss until the captain returned.

~

Another day carried Brandon closer to Crane's decision.

Death, or worse.

Brandon hoped for death, because the chance that worse could land him at the Dark Master's feet made his blood boil, fear spiking in his chest.

The captain tapped his foot impatiently, head cocked as Brandon remained still. No words had passed his lips since Crane's return approximately twenty-four hours later. Clouds covered the sun, dimming the light that shone through from the deck above, but Brandon's sense of time wasn't askew enough to confuse him.

He'd counted the hours while drowning in his thoughts.

"I have other ways to get answers from you, knight," Crane said, perching his chin on his hand. Once again, he sat in front of the cell, one leg spread before him, the other close to his chest, elbow resting on his knee. Informal, yet it gave Brandon a clear view of the sword dangling from the man's hip.

When Brandon didn't respond, the captain sighed and rose. "I've learnt much about you." He spared Brandon a glance. "I have a witch aboard. She found out that you're the lap-dog of the Ecix. Maybe you warm her bed, too."

The commander tensed at the mention of Eliza. "Do not speak of her."

The captain's brow raised. "She's set to marry Prince Alicsar. The lost prince of Cadira and the all-powerful Ecix." A laugh bubbled from his lips. "The stuff of legends. That Cadiran king certainly knows how to spin a tale for the ages."

Brandon clenched his jaw. "I cannot give you what you desire."

"Oh?" Crane stopped. "But she can."

Blood pounded in his ears as Brandon leapt to his feet. He dove for the captain, using what strength he had to rip through the charms and curl his fist into Crane's shirt and slam him into the bars of the cell.

"If you go near her," Brandon growled, "I will not hesitate to tear you apart."

Captain Crane narrowed his eyes. Before he could respond, shouts sounded above them, the scrape of metal, the loud *bang* of a cannon.

Crane ripped himself from Brandon's grasp and stumbled back.

The first ball hit the water. Above their heads, the crew yelled; for their captain, for their own cannons, and for their gods.

The second crashed into a mast; the ship rocked at the impact, sending Brandon and the captain flying.

Captain Crane leapt to his feet, swearing, pulling free Brandon's sword as he rushed to the ladder leading above deck.

Brandon waited with bated breath.

A third ball sang through the air.

It shot through the wall beside him, destroying the cell, breaking the charms keeping him locked within.

A whisper of fresh air tickled the back of his neck.

He was free.

4

CANNON FIRE

Brandon waited until the ringing in his ears subsided before ducking through the gaping hole of his cell.

He stumbled as another cannon fired, the ball singing through the air. The ship rocked on waves that crashed through the yawning hole in the belly of the ship.

Brandon looked down; water rose up his ankles, filling the room, lapping at the crates and bars that surrounded him. When he turned to stare out at sea, he found himself face to face with an enemy cannon and a ship smaller than the one he stood on.

Bloody pirates. Of course, he'd been caught in the middle of their war.

The ship looked like it might have been a Cadiran naval vessel, but the ship's name and the Cadiran crest had since been cleaned away, replaced with *The Voyager*. The vessel had three towering masts and five cannons aimed at Crane's ship. But it was not built for war, rather to cut through the waves faster than enemy ships, to carry more than just weapons and soldiers.

He hadn't seen a ship like it in years.

The water at his feet had risen in the moments he'd stopped to take in the second ship. His boots were water-logged, pants wet to his calves. The ship was going to sink and him with it if he didn't move. Debris floated around him, the remnants of onions and potatoes bobbing past. The storm outside grew heavier, darker. In the distance, lightning illuminated the clouds, crossing the skies.

Another ball exploded from a cannon, drowning out the rumble of thunder.

Brandon ducked his head as he waded over to the table where his satchel and a number of his weapons had been discarded. The boat rocked again with the impact of another canon, almost sending him down into the rising water.

The belongings that were left weren't valuable; a couple of daggers, some no bigger than the palm of his hand, a map of the eastern coast of Laziroth, rations and a water-skin. He had only the essentials in his satchel, and his chain...

Brandon reached a hand to his throat and touched the cold silver that circled his neck. Isolde's chain was still there. He released a breath. He'd never been more thankful for magic than he was in that moment, thankful for Celia, who had charmed it so only she, Brandon, and Eliza could see it.

He dropped his hand, gathered his belongings, and climbed.

The hatch above his head opened; he expected some kind of give, expected the mast to have fallen upon it, but it swung open. A breath of relief slipped from his lips.

Brandon climbed up and into the fight.

~

Blood mixed with the salty ocean spray as he ducked the attack of a pirate. Brandon shoved the sunburnt man back, didn't wince as he fell overboard and into the dark ocean that threatened to claim Crane's ship.

Brandon searched the deck as another cannon exploded, crashing into the deck mere feet from where he stood. Crane's ship was the larger of the two, and it was going under—fast.

Pirates filled the top deck, a mess of bodies and blood, fighting against the sinking ship for control. Above Brandon, lithe bodies swung between vessels; those from the second ship swarmed

Crane's crew, but Brandon couldn't tell who belonged to which captain.

But he needed to find Crane, needed his sword.

"You." Brandon spun and found himself face to face with a younger pirate; his shirt was open, revealing a red chest, bloodied and bruised, a strap of leather crossing the wounds on his skin. The young man pulled a cutlass free. "You should be below deck."

One of Crane's then, Brandon thought, flexing his fingers. He palmed a dagger. The young man grinned, like he'd already won the fight.

But Brandon was better with a dagger. He'd learnt long ago that some of the easiest kills came with a smaller blade.

He let the young pirate attack first; ducking the first blow, Brandon spun out of the way of the next, staying quick on his feet despite the blood threatening to put him on his ass. It coated the deck like rain.

But the pirate wasn't as quick—or careful. He fell, head slamming into the wood. For a moment, he lay there, eyes wide.

Brandon swept up the man's discarded cutlass and pressed the tip of the blade into the boy's throat. "Stay down."

Fear flashed across his bright eyes, but it didn't stop him from scrambling back and rising.

One sweep of Brandon's hand, and the pirate fell, bright eyes going dim as the slice through his throat grew bloody. Brandon wiped the blade clean and held onto it. His stomach churned, but he turned from the body and the blood that fell between the cracked deck. Brandon searched the sea of bodies for the captain.

Brandon wondered if Crane had already gone overboard, if maybe the raging ocean had claimed his blade. It was one of the few things he had left from Isolde, a gift before the war.

He never went anywhere without it.

And he certainly wasn't going to start now.

Brandon spied dark locs and a flash of steel, the head of a raven clutched in the hands of a pirate.

Crane fought well, Brandon would give him that. Perhaps, once long ago, he'd been a soldier himself. There was a methodical way to how he moved, to the glide of the blade as it sang through the air.

But the one he battled was better.

They fought at the bow of the ship, where the battle was at its thickest. Brandon stood near the mainmast, which had splintering cracks that threatened to topple it.

Brandon entered the fray; he ducked blades, sidestepped falling bodies. The deck wasn't designed to hold so many men at once, thrown together in battle, swinging cutlasses and axes. As he avoided the cut of blades and punches, Brandon set his sight on the next step. His only purpose was to get his sword back from Crane, then maybe he would beg for passage on the other ship.

A body slammed into his, knocking Brandon back several steps and into the warm body of a surly man who threw him forward. Brandon stumbled and righted himself before he could be pushed into the water, the ship's railing bobbing in the dark abyss below.

As he looked up, the pirate glared at him and spat, "Stupid fuckin' knight." The smell of alcohol wafted off the man, darkening his breath.

Brandon clenched his jaw as the pirate swung, aiming for Brandon's throat, but the commander danced out of reach. The pirate's movements were sloppy and slow, riddled with mistakes that should have killed him long ago. It was his size that made him a worthy opponent—not skill.

At least it made it easy for Brandon to stay out of reach.

The pirate, bored after a few lazy swings, turned away from Brandon and set his sights on another. For a moment, the commander was thankful for the distraction, but he watched as the pirate aimed for the back of a dark-haired boy, no older than Eliza, who was too busy fighting off another of Crane's men to notice the attack from behind.

Brandon rushed the pirate as his blade pierced the skin of the boy. Blood boiled with the magic of the witches, thrumming in Brandon's ears as he pushed the drunk aside, freeing the boy from his grasp. The cutlass fell from Brandon's grip, and he let it drop to the blood-soaked deck, preferring one of his daggers instead.

The boy stumbled aside. But the drunk lost his balance, knocking down a woman behind him as he righted himself. A growl tore from his chest, but Brandon flipped the blade in his hand, a grim smile etched across his lips.

The boy offered Brandon a smile as the drunk pirate rushed

towards him.

Brandon ducked and sliced through the abdomen of Crane's man, rising in one fluid motion. The boy planted a kick in the centre of the drunk's chest, sending him to the dark depths below.

The boy heaved a breath, looked at Brandon, and bowed his head. Then he was gone, taking a rope in one hand, his cutlass in the other, and swung over to the second ship.

~

Brandon found Crane with a knife to his throat, and a young woman at the other end of it.

The tips of her blonde-white hair were dyed red with the blood of her enemy. The dark leather of her pants and the milky skin of her hands stained crimson, but otherwise she looked untouched.

Sucking in a breath, Brandon spied his sword at Crane's feet. His heart leapt into his throat.

The captain of the sinking ship started laughing. "You know, if you weren't a bitch, I would commend you on this take over," he said, meeting the woman's eye. "But you won't get away with—"

She pressed the dagger harder against his windpipe, cutting him off. "I already have," she whispered.

Brandon waited to see if she'd slit his throat, but instead she slammed the hilt into the side of Crane's head. Crane fell at her feet, and she kicked him once in the groin before bending down to unclip the pistol at his hip.

She considered it a moment before saying, "Speak, before I blow your brains out." The woman lifted a brow and spun, pressing the nozzle into Brandon's skull.

Around them, the fighting came to a standstill. Weapons were dropped to the bloody deck, cannons cooled, and those with the female captain held the remainder of Crane's crew at knife point.

Brandon might have been impressed if it weren't for the weapon and the woman threatening to kill him. He had met very few female captains, especially ones who could best someone like Crane throughout his years.

Eliza would have liked her, he thought, as bitter guilt filled his mouth.

The dagger he held clattered to the ground. "I'm not with Crane or his crew."

Something clicked inside the pistol; the woman let a small smile flicker across her plump lips. "Oh? And who might you be, then?"

Brandon looked between her, the sword at her feet, and the burning vessel sinking into the ocean. "I am Brandon Thorne of the Brotherhood, a commander of King Bastian's army, and close confidant of the Ecix."

The woman in front of him narrowed her eyes; two sets of hands ripped him back, taking his arms and forcing them behind his back. He didn't resist.

"Why did Crane want you?" she asked, eyes narrowing as she took him in. Her gaze was like fire as it slid down his body.

No questioning of who he claimed to be... he should have sensed it earlier, the tinge of Blood Magic in the air. It crawled across his skin, kin calling to kin.

She'd been touched by Blood Magic. Unease worked its way through him, heavy and thick.

Brandon pressed his lips into a thin line and cast the fallen captain a look. "Wanted what most idiot mortals want."

The woman snorted and shook her head. "The immortality of the witches." She raised a brow. "And you were stupid enough to get captured?" The hand holding the pistol dropped, no longer pointed at his head, but she took a step forward.

"I have no issue with you or your people. All I need is passage."

"To where?" she asked quietly.

He looked between her and the ship bobbing not far from where they sank. "Laziroth."

"Cap—" one of his captors started, but she held up a hand.

At least he was sure who he was dealing with.

"Give me one good reason why I shouldn't kill you now? I doubt the Blood Witches will care about one little knight. Surely they have plenty more."

Brandon pursed his lips, prepared to tell her about the Ecix, the threat of war, but before he could open his mouth, another voice spoke up.

"He saved my life."

The two holding Brandon wrenched him around; the boy he'd helped took a step forward, his hands clasped in front of him. He looked smaller, surrounded by his crew, but bolder. As though he felt safe enough to speak out to his captain.

"He could 'ave let me die," he said, "but he helped me. I owe him a life debt, Cap."

For a moment, the captain considered the young man, then Brandon. He couldn't read her; she could be contemplating whether it was worth keeping either of them, or she could be considering Brandon's life.

Her gaze slid from him to the pistol in her hand. She weighed it like an opportunity she could not pass up.

Brandon held his breath, preparing himself for a fight, but instead she nodded and pivoted to meet Brandon's eye. "Captain Piper," she said, nodding once at the two men holding him.

They released Brandon, shoving him with the intention of watching him fall—he dug his heels in, scowling, and straightened. He let his gaze fall to the sword—the only treasure he needed.

The captain followed his gaze, and a smile slipped upon her lips. She looked him over before holstering the pistol and kicking him the sword. "Welcome to the *Voyager*, Commander Thorne."

5

CAPTAIN PIPER

Once they were safely on the deck of Captain Piper's ship, three final explosions went off. The ship rocked with the impact. Brandon watched as the balls collided with the remnants of Crane's vessel, where he and his crew sank into the depths of the Goddesses domain.

Brandon swallowed a prayer to the sea goddess, but knew she would not hear him.

He looked to the captain, who stood beside him, her white-blonde hair billowing around her head. She was almost as tall as him, her frame lean, skin tanned from time spent in the harsh sun. She likely spent most of her days on the northern coasts of Laziroth and Cadira, where the seas were untested and unmatched, where sirens sang their sultry tunes and led men to their deaths.

"You're staring," she said to him, turning away from the sinking ship. To the crew, she shouted, "Prepare to depart! Start mending the holes and make sure those sails aren't torn."

From the corner of his eye, Brandon watched the young boy he'd saved scurry for the mainmast, where he climbed hooks so easily Brandon wondered if he'd been born to do so.

The captain took a step, then over her shoulder said, "Follow me."

Brandon wasn't in a place to argue; several people, a mixture of men and women, all watched him with keen, weary eyes. They didn't trust him, and he didn't trust them, either.

But he followed the captain up to the helm, where the helmsman bowed their head and disappeared.

Captain Piper took the wheel and pursed her lips. "So you want to go to Laziroth," she mused, keeping her eyes on the horizon.

Brandon spared a glance at the almost submerged ship. "Yes."

"Why?"

He tensed. Though he should have expected it, it still caught him off guard. "I'm on a mission," he replied. If he kept his answers vague, then he ran less of a risk of putting his friends in danger should Captain Piper turn out to be worse than Crane. He wouldn't risk his mission further.

The captain shook her head. A man approached; he'd been one of the pair responsible for grabbing Brandon, though now that he stood in front of the commander, he could finally take in the tall, bronze-skinned Lazirothian pirate.

A head taller than both Brandon and Piper, he had the broad shoulders of someone from the mountain regions of Laziroth, onyx-black hair, and equally dark eyes. A born warrior was how Brandon's brothers would describe him. Brows drawn in concern, his darks eyes flickered from Brandon to his captain.

"Captain," he said, turning to Piper. "Are you sure about this?"

There was a hint of concern in his voice. Brandon crossed his arms, eyed the two of them as they shared a glance.

"Are you sure about helping *him*?" the man asked.

For a moment, the captain stood there, staring up at him. Something passed in her gaze; Brandon touched the pommel of his sword cautiously, thankful she'd returned it to him, but wary of her motives.

Piper cut Brandon a glance and sighed. "I'll take you to Laziroth." She looked back up at her friend. "Question me again, Osiris, and I *will* drop your ass in K'ahryan Bay with the flesh eaters, understood?"

Osiris sighed and shook his head. "Aye, Cap. Understood."

Captain Piper turned her gaze on Brandon and pressed her lips into a line. "Unless there's something else you need, Knight, you can leave."

The commander blinked, then bowed his head. He turned on his heel without another word and quickly descended onto the main deck. A pull in his gut stopped him from entering the ferocious storm of rebuilding, and instead, he slipped into the shadows beneath the quarterdeck.

"I still don't understand what we need in Laziroth," Osiris said.

"I'll explain tonight." There was a pause, but the voices of the crew drowned out the rest.

After another quiet moment, Brandon considered slipping away, but her voice rang out once more. "Hoist the sails!" she shouted. "To Laziroth we go!"

~

The further west they sailed, the air—and the water that carried them—grew warmer. Brandon remained above deck, rather than joining the rest of the crew below. Though they hadn't voiced their disapproval of his addition, he'd felt the disdainful stares, heard the snide comments thrown in his directions.

Brandon didn't blame them, and the last thing he wanted was to make them uncomfortable. So he perched himself on the forecastle, overlooking the waves and bowsprit pointing towards the coast of Laziroth.

He closed his eyes and leaned back against the railing. If he listened hard enough, would he hear the song of sirens, or the battle of mermaids seeking shelter from the onslaught of dark magic filling their oceans?

Or would he lose himself to his own thoughts once more, as he grew further from Eliza and Cadira, from Celia and Amitel, and the fear that perhaps they'd made a mistake in letting Alicsar live?

Brandon opened his eyes and let a shuddering breath pass his lips. Rising, he took in the rest of the ship; a small woman stood at the helm, her dark eyes glued to the horizon, ignoring him. Nestled in the crow's nest, neither looking towards the horizon nor at Brandon, the boy who had spoken up for him in front of Captain Piper. Brandon had watched him scamper up there earlier, and the boy had yet to return.

Other than those above deck, Brandon was alone.

Captain Piper and Osiris had taken their leave early in the evening. The door to the captain's quarters was beneath the quarterdeck, outlined by two stained glass windows featuring a mountain range.

A sense of unease settled deep in Brandon's gut. He rose and started down to the main deck, sparing the young woman a quick glance, but she didn't look away from the horizon.

Brandon stopped and crouched outside the small door that led into the captain's quarters. The voices that carried were almost clear in the quiet night.

Someone slammed their hand into a table, the rattling of coins and other metal objects clear through the low, stained glass window that overlooked the deck. "We've one chance left with the High Lords, Pip. If we want to go back—"

"We have the Erkis pistol now, Osiris," she replied. "We don't need the High Lords when we can take them all out with this."

Brandon frowned and thought back to Crane's pistol. It hadn't seemed all that powerful, and as he tried to wrack his brain for any information about pistols, Piper continued, voice hushed.

"We need to go to Laziroth if we want to find it before anyone else can."

For a moment, Osiris was quiet. Then, tired, he asked, "Did you know Crane had the pistol?"

"Gods no." She scoffed. "And I've no clue how he got this, either. But it's ours now, and we can finally change our fates."

Another moment of silence passed. Brandon pushed away, pressing his lips together as he slipped out of the shadows and into the moon's line of sight. It soaked the deck in its silver light, reflecting off the dark ocean that surrounded him.

He hadn't expected to overhear talk of a pistol. What he'd expected was talk of his inevitable death, or perhaps selling him off to the highest bidder, perhaps even continuing what Crane started.

He knew nothing of an Erkis pistol, so he slipped that piece of knowledge into the back of his mind for later, a gift for Eliza should she even want to speak to him again when he returned.

But Brandon knew of the High Lords. They weren't true

nobility, not in the sense of what Cadira had. Who he assumed Piper and Osiris spoke of were the High Pirate Lords, twelve pirates who have sailed the seas of the Shadowland and who each came from one of the twelve major oceans and coasts.

If Piper and her crew were outcasts from the High Lords, what did that mean for him?

Brandon tucked that knowledge away, too, as he returned to his perch on the forecastle.

6

BEFORE

Brandon and Amitel circled Enya's establishment twice before laying their trap; with fire gathered from burning embers circling the dock, they coaxed it into a living creature that engulfed the air and threatened to grow. With the help of Amitel's waning magic, they smothered it just enough so they could climb above the mercenaries and the houses, where they would drop the flame on to the weakened planks below and destroy the dock—the mercenaries along with it.

Behind him, Amitel swore. Brandon cast a quick glance back at the warlock to find the flame already growing. The closer they got to the establishment, the faster it flourished. Below them, the mercenaries were none the wiser, but if Amitel couldn't get the fire under control, they'd be shot down from the ropes holding them and would surely drown in the burning water below.

They just needed to hold on a few more moments.

Brandon climbed to the other side and reached for the flame as it leapt at Amitel's hand; the warlock cursed and handed it off before shaking away the fire that circled his wrist. The flesh around the cuff of his shirt turned pink, but disappeared—likely under a glamour, or healed with magic.

Amitel joined him, and stared at the fire. "Let's get this over with," he muttered, cradling the burnt hand to his chest. They stood on the sill of a window, huddled close together.

Brandon watched Amitel from the corner of his eye. "Do you trust me?"

Amitel blinked, lips pressed into a line. "Enough."

Brandon nodded and held out the torch as the flame grew once more. It leapt at his own fingers, but he threw it to the dock, and watched with bated breath as it landed on the exposed wood, and exploded.

They shielded their faces, but only had moments to get down before their cover was revealed. Brandon took the rope, grabbed Amitel, and palmed a dagger. He flipped it once, so the blade was between his fingers, then aimed for the house across from them, where the rope was tied to another windowsill. Knocking the dagger back, Brandon released it.

The dagger sliced through the weakened thread of the rope. As it released, he and Amitel jumped from their perch and let the rope guide them safely to the door.

As they came down, Brandon pushed off the wall, dropped Amitel, and bent his knees for impact with the door. His bloody boots slammed into the wood, snapping it at the hinges.

Brandon dropped, unsheathed his sword, and entered the house.

~

She was waiting for them at her desk, men on either side of her, feet thrown up and crossed at the ankles. A smug little grin pinched her thin, pink lips. Soot darkened the red of her hair, and her pale skin looked sickly in the light.

The screams of her dying men disappeared as they crossed the threshold.

Enya clapped her hands slowly. "Well done. You found me." She kicked off the desk and rose. "But the creature isn't here."

Brandon's grip tightened on his sword. "Where is she, Enya?"

She cocked her head and pouted. "I'm not talking to you, soldier boy." Her watery-blue eyes snapped to Amitel. "But I'll listen to you, lover boy... maybe."

The warlock's eyes narrowed. "Where is the oracle?"

"Already on her way out of town." Enya circled the desk so she could stand before them, revealing burns that laced her hands and arms, undressed and uncovered, open for them to see. She didn't wince or even acknowledge the pain. "I just wanted to stick around and wait for you to finally catch up. And to make sure you definitely don't make it out of here alive."

Brandon clenched his jaw. "We'll stop you."

"I doubt it," she replied as the back door slammed open. Five burly men and women stormed the room, armed to the teeth with an array of what Brandon assumed were stolen weapons; dragon bone swords, daggers forged by the Brotherhood, several more blades that otherwise shouldn't be in the hands of thieves and killers. "You two are trapped. If you haven't noticed, there's a boundary spell circling the building that's put a little stop on Amitel's magic."

Brandon spared the warlock a quick glance, only to find Amitel's fingers twitching with a spell, hopefully one that would unravel the magic around them. It explained Amitel's brief fumble with the flame, why he couldn't take out the mercenaries on his own. But Brandon couldn't feel the warlock's magic.

Brandon hoped it was because of the fire, that it was stifling even the smallest trace, and not because of Enya's spell.

"You two were smart, destroying the dock. And I hear you've been ferrying lost souls out of the village. How noble of you." She shook her head, wild red hair bouncing around the subtle points of her ears. "It's too bad my men have orders to burn either side of the lake once we're done."

"And risk the fire following you?" Amitel asked. "Are you that naïve? It'll burn until all is consumed."

"It'll burn until the last life has been taken." She rolled her eyes. "Beyond the village, there is little to no human life for the fire to take. Once we're out of reach, it'll burn out."

Brandon shook his head. "You have no care for all those that have already been lost. And for what? A small glimpse at the future?"

"You saw the war, did you not, knight of the Brotherhood?" she asked. Brandon's heart leapt into his throat. "You saw the destruction the shadow creature caused, how it killed the one being that should be as powerful as a god?" Enya took a step forward; Brandon's heart cracked in his chest at the mention of Isolde. "Wouldn't you have liked the chance to stop that? To even have an idea of what might be coming?"

Enya looked him over with crazed eyes. "The oracle has already revealed much to me about the collective future of our world. That darkness from the north will come again, and it will grow stronger. It will consume everything in its path and start a war that will destroy everything we know."

"And you believe the oracle?" Amitel asked. Enya's gaze snapped to his, frenzied eyes narrowed in frustration. "You truly think the oracle is telling you the truth?"

"Why wouldn't she?" Enya took a step forward, and the crossbows of all her people rose to rest on the thundering hearts of Brandon and Amitel. "The future could be stopped. She said that. She said the future isn't set."

"Oracles spin little stories to stop you from killing them." Amitel took a step forward. "You never took stock in this before. Why now? What's so important that you would kill hundreds of innocents?"

Enya said nothing as she circled the desk. She stopped and rifled through a drawer, her narrowed eyes focused on the rapid movements of her hands, and not them.

Brandon would have tried to strike, were it not for the five mercenaries glaring at him. Their crossbows lifted a little higher in anticipation, but they didn't release the thick bolts aimed at the pairs' chests.

He considered Amitel's words as he glared at the young woman, who seemed too engrossed in her own head to even care that they were still standing there. What had the oracle said to her to scare her?

What had been revealed that warranted so much destruction? So much death?

"Ah." She lifted her head, producing a rolled piece of parchment, no larger than his pinkie finger. As she unrolled it, she let a small, bitter smile unfurl across her lips. "I, Queen Asteria of the Dream Court, hereby denounce Enya of the Chosen and banish her from the Courts of Light. From this day until her last, Enya of the Chosen can no longer cross the boundary into the Courts. To do so will forfeit her life." Enya looked up from the parchment, the smile gone from her lips. A darkness filled her eyes as she stepped away from the desk. "I tried to warn Asteria of what was coming, you know."

Brandon frowned, eyes flickering from her to the crossbows. "What do you mean?"

"The war..." She dragged her fingers over the wood of the desk as she rounded it once more. "I've always had... premonitions." She looked up to meet Amitel's eye, like she sought solace in his gaze. But when Brandon looked over at his companion, he found the warlock's harsh stare on the desk. When Brandon looked back, he found Enya looking down at her scarred hands.

"She didn't believe me. The Queen of Dreams didn't believe what I'd seen in my nightmares." Enya closed her hands into fists, the raw skin bleeding as she did. "So I needed to find someone she would believe. I needed to find an oracle."

Brandon and Amitel shared a look as Enya started for a back door, picking up the letter as she did. Over her shoulder, she spared them a look, and said, "I'm sorry it had to come to this. I only needed you to find it. I never wanted you to die for the truth."

The mercenaries surrounding them took a step forward, their fingers moving to the trigger. The blood in Brandon's veins thrummed, boiling as Enya slipped through the door, followed by two of her men.

Leaving them to die.

7

LAZIROTH

In the darkness of dawn, the outline of the shore appeared, highlighted by the rising Cadiran sun. They'd made good time, though Brandon had expected storms to ravage the sea between Cadira and Laziroth. But it had been smooth, almost like the Goddess Adira and her twin, Alon, were friends for the first time in centuries.

The repairs to the ship had been made efficiently, with no argument from Brandon as Captain Piper set him to work to mend a mast, claiming his *added strength* would make the job easier. Though Brandon hadn't appreciated her setting him against her crew, they'd managed to do the repairs without a word uttered, and he'd been given a hammock below deck to call his own until they made it to the coast of Laziroth.

But most nights he remained above deck, where he could see the ocean and the horizon, where he could sleep in solitude with only the boy in the crow's nest and the girl at the helm.

Brandon straightened against the railing as several of the crew watched him closely. In only a short couple of hours, he'd be gone, and he'd never have to see the crew again.

Reaching up to his throat, Brandon clasped a hand around the chain he wore. Memories of Isolde threatened to cut through him. He'd done well in the two hundred years since her death to block her out, but it had been hard since meeting Eliza. And it was hard not being in her presence, to not feel like he was close to Isolde while being by Eliza's side. It grew like an ache in his chest, burrowing deep into his bones.

He released a heavy breath. More of the crew clambered on deck, rushing to prepare for port. It wasn't large, likely not an established trading post from what he could tell, but there was still an air of unease that spread along the crew. Piper likely had fake documents claiming her vessel was a trading one—that, or the people of the seaside village didn't care that pirates were stopping. If they made coin, then he supposed it didn't matter.

As a knight of the Brotherhood, he didn't care. Pirates were pirates; they would exist so long as there were seas to sail and towns to pillage, gold and gems to steal, and ships to call home.

The commander of the Cadiran army, however, battled internally with what they were doing. Part of him feared they would pillage and kill the town they were docking in.

He shook his head. *This is nothing you can stop*, he thought. *And this isn't why you're here.*

The noise of the deck turned to silence. He turned towards the helmsman's quarters, where Captain Piper stood, her arms crossed. She looked less pirate and more tradesman with her striking white-blonde hair pulled back into a knot at the nape of her neck, a dark mahogany tailored coat over her black breeches and white tunic. The sword at her side, however, was practical and not ornamental like most traders wore, the grip and pommel worn down with age, yet still polished to a shine. The blade was smaller, like one a child might learn with, but the lightweight nature of it would serve the captain well in battle, he imagined.

Brandon turned from her and cast his gaze over the horizon. Once, when dragons had roamed freely over Laziroth and most other lands, there had been sea beasts the size of three naval blockade vessels. He'd never seen them, but once, as a young boy, he and a friend had stumbled across the skull of one in a sea cave close to his village. It had disappeared a week later.

Warlocks, he later learned, were always collecting the bones of dragons. It had something to do with their magic. Brandon had never asked Amitel, and part of him didn't want to know.

The captain stopped at his side, but she didn't look at him. Her youth surprised Brandon. There was a hardness to her features that told him she was a woman, but her eyes told the story of a young girl who'd seen too much in her short life.

That same tingle of Blood Magic he'd felt the first time they'd met slid along his skin, turning the hairs on his arms up.

They stood in silence as the crew worked quickly for docking. The town gradually grew larger, filling the horizon. The houses were mud and stone, some with thatched roofs while others sat on stilts over the water. There were maybe five fishing boats bobbing close by, though the coast they'd sailed to was further north than he'd expected. For it, he was thankful.

A dockmaster waved them down as the crew steadied the *Voyager* to a slow stop.

The captain produced something from her jacket pocket, a small crystal the colour of a Cadiran sunset. "Here," she said, handing it to him. It weighed no more than seashell. "If you are in need of aid, you can use this to call me."

Brandon stared at the crystal, then at the young-woman. "I—"

She held up her hand, scowling. "I have no interest in you, Brotherhood."

He blinked as her eyes narrowed. He had expected nothing of her, and yet she defied his expectations every time. Perhaps they were kin with their Blood Magic, or perhaps she knew more than she let on. Regardless, he was thankful.

"Oh."

Her scowl transformed into a smirk. "Unless you're hiding lady parts beneath those boring travel pants, you are not my type."

Heat rushed up his neck, and he forced himself to look away. Clearing his throat, he pocketed the item. "Then why?"

She shrugged. "You intrigue me." There was something else in her stare as their eyes met, something he couldn't quite read. "But I hope you will not speak a word of me or my crew to those you serve."

"You have my word." He didn't question the command. Any curiosity he had quickly vanished. It wasn't his secret to learn; if she wanted him to know why, then she would tell him.

As she turned to step away, she paused. "I have one more question for you, knight."

He raised a brow. "Anything."

"Your kind... the Brotherhood." She paused, and her gaze went up to the crow's nest, where the boy peaked his head over and watched the two of them with wide eyes. "When do they take initiates?"

Brandon took a step back and cut Piper a quick glance. Of all the questions, he hadn't expected that one. "Why?"

"Taggy's brother left. Disappeared during our last stop in Cadira." She looked over her shoulder and met Brandon's stare. The boy—Taggy—slipped into the crow's nest, no longer visible to either of them. "He had this grand idea that he should become one of the Brotherhood. A knight for the witches."

The *Idrindis* was the ceremony where the Brotherhood gathered its new recruits and the witches found fathers for the next generation of Blood Witches. It encompassed weeks of trials and celebrations that masked the true nature of the holiday.

"When?" he asked.

"Three weeks ago." She looked down at her hands, then back up at him. "What happens to the boys who don't make it?"

Brandon had been a naïve boy when he'd accepted the summons to compete. There had been rounds of exhausting trials to weed out those undeserving of immortality, and even if they made it in the eyes of captains—the men who lead the knights—the final say went to the Blood Witches.

Some had said Isolde had been his saving grace.

And to that, he agreed.

If it weren't for her selecting him during the *Idrindis*, he likely wouldn't have survived.

"Death is what I was told," he finally replied. "Excruciating death."

The captain pursed her lips. "I hope for his sake that he survives."

"I hope so too." The witches would be planning their next ceremony, especially with the return of Eliza. And they would want her there, to oversee the ceremony, like Isolde had for her generation.

The coastline was closer now, and the salty brine of the coast grew stronger with it.

"Thank you." Captain Piper held out her hand, and he grasped it tightly. "Safe travels," she said.

He gave her a half-smile. "And you."

When he stepped off the dreaded *Voyager*, he almost considered throwing the crystal into the waters of Laziroth. But a nagging voice—Celia's, if he were being honest—told him not to. That perhaps the pirate might be useful in the war to come.

As he walked alone up the docks, he pocketed the crystal once again, with hopes that he might just find what he needed in the land of dragons.

8

VARUN

The dragons of Laziroth were almost gone; those that remained were hidden around the world where Hunters—fierce warriors born in the heartland of Laziroth and bred to seek out Riders—couldn't find them.

In all his years, Brandon had yet to meet a Dragon or its Rider. As a boy, it had been his dream to see one of the noble beasts up close, but it had soon been washed away, and he kept that dream locked deep within him.

In the years since the Great Dragon Hunts, most of Laziroth learned to condemn those born with the ability to ride dragons. They had been perhaps the best allies to have in case of war, but since the hunt began, almost an entire culture had been destroyed.

Brandon kept thoughts of dragons to himself as he climbed another incline. The memory of the waterside village he and Amitel had visited years ago was murky, but the magic that came with being one of the Brotherhood meant he could access those memories. Being away from the magic of the Blood Witches, however, meant he wasn't as strong as his brothers, that those abilities he took for granted weakened with his time away from the witches.

He stopped and gazed over the village of Varun; Amitel had explained to him during their first visit how the village had been named after one of the Lazirothian Gods of the sea and ocean—though because of how large the continent was, there were many deities, and the God Varun had many legends.

The village looked larger than the last time Brandon had seen it; perched atop a large lake, the houses and businesses now spread further towards the land, more fishing vessels dotting the water, vanishing down the large river that emptied out into the ocean. The village surrounded a drowned cathedral styled building that was built before the lake itself, with catacombs lost to the water, serving as a graveyard for the souls left behind.

Brandon's thoughts went to Eliza, and how she'd find it fascinating.

Stop it, he thought, shaking his head. He needed to stop dwelling on Eliza, on what he'd done. The oracle, the little girl who had spewed songs of fate, could answer his questions, so he could return to Eliza with more than empty promises.

With skilled fingers, he locked away thoughts of Eliza. He refused to dwell on how easy it was, that over time he'd become an expert in hiding feelings and memories away. He wanted to blame the Brotherhood and his training, but after two hundred years, he knew it had more to do with himself than what others did to him.

It was easier to lock it away than think about it.

Brandon followed the road down to the village, where a ferry service operated, taking people and carts from the shore to the docks of Varun. The ferry service crossed the lake itself to the other side, where a thin road led into the mountain range surrounding the village.

He would need to follow it inland, where the terrain grew mountainous, unsafe, and rarely travelled. It would take him days to reach the valley where the temple of the Oracle was hidden, the hike alone exhausting for humans, but he hoped, despite his time away from the Blood Witches, he was strong enough to make it there sooner.

Before he could travel that way, he'd need to stop and rest, gather supplies. He had no idea if the oracle was even there still. He hoped she was—prayed to the Goddess that in the two hundred years since being in Laziroth, the oracle hadn't been taken.

Farmers waited to take the ferry, but as mid-day rolled around—and the sun burned the back of Brandon's neck—the commander found himself atop the water with a young mother and her two children, an old fisherman who only fished at the water's edge, and two men who made Brandon reach for the pommel of his sword as they shared a dark look. The commander kept a wary eye on them, even as they docked, and he paid the ferry toll.

The two men walked in the direction of the cathedral, disappearing down a dark alley. Brandon made sure to go in the opposite direction.

Even with the village's expansion, he found himself walking down a familiar path. The rotten wood creaked an old, forgotten song, the gentle lull of the lake accompanying the tune. He'd been a broken man with a shattered heart, searching for some semblance of the life he'd once known the last time in he'd been to Varun.

Brandon paused and shoved his hand into his pockets. The house that had once belonged to Amitel's old friend was no longer standing, burnt down along with most of the village almost two hundred years ago. A pang of guilt shot through him as he stared down into the murky depths where the ruins likely slept on the lake's floor.

He shook his head and continued. Stopping would make him suspicious. There were guards now, where there hadn't been years ago. Although the structures looked the same, the air of Varun was different, filled with tension he only now felt as he walked the slippery streets.

A tavern with a swinging sign appeared. There was little sound coming from within, so hiding would be difficult, but many were likely working away on boats and the surrounding farms, or building ships and houses to fit the influx of civilians. Those who sat around tables drinking and eating were either too old to work, or were in Varun for different reasons.

Unlike most of the village, the tavern was a stone building that had likely withstood the flooding of the original valley that now held the lake and its floating city. It had survived his last appearance, which brought a smile to Brandon's lips. Its dark exterior descended into the murky water, the stone a slick green where the lake claimed it.

Brandon entered and sucked in a breath. The watery brine followed him, but as the door closed, he found himself wrapped in the warmth of the kitchen and the spices local to Laziroth. Taking a seat at the bar, Brandon kept an eye on the door. The man working the tavern looked up at him with dark eyes and a frown.

"What'll it be?" the bartender asked, voice hoarse.

Brandon spared him a glance; he had the dark brown skin of most Lazirothian people, though his was dried and leathered from years of working in the sun.

Looking away, Brandon spied a group of approaching men. They wore leathers around their broad chests and abdomens, but their thick uncovered biceps revealed tattoos that slid down their right arms and over their hands.

"I wouldn't stare," the barkeep muttered. When Brandon looked at him again, he noticed the flash of fear in the man's dark eyes. "They don't like it when stranger's stare."

"They're Dragon Hunters," Brandon said. He recognised the insignia on their arms; two curved blades formed an 'x', fire forming a ring around them. In one of Laziroth's mother tongues, there was only one word on the tattoo: hunt. It was nothing fancy or original, but the symbol sparked fear into anyone who dared harbour the beasts and their riders. Crane's vest had been of a similar, disturbing make.

The leather, Brandon realised as the group stalked closer, was made out of dragonhide, which he vaguely remembered was usually reserved for skilled riders. Hunters wore a style similar to the paintings of riders he'd seen, only looking upon them now, he realised how grotesque and offensive it was.

Shaking his head, Brandon pulled a small purse from his pocket and slid two silver coins to the barkeep. "One for a room and food, and another for your silence."

The barkeep, stunned, gave a slight nod of his head. "Of course."

Without hesitation, he pocketed the coins and retrieved a key. "Upstairs, third door on your left. I'll have someone bring hot water up for you, and a hot meal, if you don't want to be with the rest of 'em."

Brandon shook his head. "I don't want to be a bother. I'll eat like everyone else." When he found the man's eyes again, he sighed. "But hot water would be appreciated greatly."

"Course."

The barkeep shouted something in a language Brandon didn't understand, and moments later, a steaming fish and crab stew sat before him, two slices of the day's bread beside it. The smell tickled the back of his nose and awaked a hunger inside him, but he ate slowly. The barkeep leaned forward, sliding Brandon a cup of sweet wine.

"The Hunters don't like strangers," he warned, eyes flickering from Brandon to the group of now seated men.

"Why are you telling me this?" Brandon asked, sipping carefully at the drink. It was tangy, something he definitely hadn't expected from Varun.

The barkeep's gaze flickered from him to the Hunters. "Let's just say, when soldiers from Cadira enter my tavern, I know it isn't for anything good."

Brandon swallowed. "I'm not here for the Hunters."

"They might be here for you, though."

The barkeep didn't say anything more as he disappeared into what Brandon thought was the kitchen, hidden behind the bar through a swinging door. He understood why a moment later, as two Hunters appeared beside him.

The one that radiated the most authority sat, while the other stood at Brandon's back. The leader had long, ebony hair, pin straight and thick. A leather tie held it back from his square face. Lines marked the skin around his lips and eyes—he was likely in his fortieth year, which Brandon admitted was impressive, given his work, but since dragons were rare, it wasn't like he was putting himself in danger often. Which either meant his presence on hunts was rare, or he was lucky.

The hunter raised a brow. "What's a Cadiran doing in Varun?" he asked, accent thick, giving Brandon a half smile. "We don't see many of your sort this far inland."

"Family," Brandon replied with a shrug. "My sister-in-law's family is in Wyre." The lie slipped from his tongue as simply as if it were the truth. Wyre, he knew, was the next major town after the location of the oracle, and had been the hometown of one of the Brotherhood's knights. They'd been part of the same *Idrindis* group when Brandon had first met Isolde.

The hunter narrowed his eyes. "Nice place."

"I've never been." Truth. "My brother is there now." Lie.

If the hunter could tell he was lying, he didn't say anything. "Then enjoy your time here in Varun." The hunter paused and touched his chin. "But I must say, it would be an awful tragedy if you were forced to miss your brother and his bride."

"I'll be gone by morning." The threat wasn't lost on Brandon, and when he picked up his cup once more, he downed it, the sweet liquid making his head foggy only for a moment before the magic of his immortality washed away the effects. "But I'll enjoy what I can before then."

"Shame," the leader said, "I would have invited you on our next hunt."

Brandon tensed as the leader and the other hunter walked away. They knew—sensed, somehow—that Brandon wasn't just Cadiran. Rumours had been floating around that in the years since the great hunts, Hunters had gained some kind of ability—likely through a magic of some sort—to sense dragons.

But the hunt likely wouldn't have been for dragons or riders. More likely a test; was the Cadiran truly in Laziroth for family, or something far more valuable?

Dragons and riders would be needed in the coming war. The Hunters knew that.

So what were they hiding?

9

HUNTED

The cool air carried with it the smell of rotten fish and river water. It usually wouldn't bother Brandon, but during his mid-day hike through Varun, with the sun beating down on him and the brown water, he couldn't help but scrunch his nose at the smell.

Fishermen called to one another while women used the edges of the docks to fill buckets of sloshing brown water. There were filters in most buildings to clean the water, as well as scattered across the village for anyone to use. But the lake carried sickness if not treated properly.

For the first time in a while, he thanked his immortality, which protected him from regular, mortal illnesses.

There were many in Varun who were sick with fevers born of the water. The growing population didn't help the weakened city, and the addition of Dragon Hunters made the people nervous. Out of curiosity—and to keep them from following him—Brandon had stayed days longer than he would have liked. He couldn't know if the oracle was still where she'd been hidden almost two hundred years ago, but he refused to give the Hunters a chance to find her.

Brandon threw a look over his shoulder and found two figures half-hidden in the shadows, watching him. He'd noticed them many times since his arrival and subsequent run-in with the leader of the Hunters. If they were his men, then Brandon knew he couldn't go far without his absence noticed.

No one questioned Brandon's prolonged stay, so he never gave a reason. The silver coins kept the tavern owner quiet, and the long nights alone gave him a chance to think about what it was he was doing, to dwell on why he'd left.

Because it hadn't just been about feeling useless at the palace. There, he could have at least trained Eliza, helped her through the marriage, through her learning with the Blood Witches.

And now he was alone. Not even Isolde appeared in his dreams, though he suspected she was staying away for the same reasons why he'd left.

Brandon turned down another alley. On either side of him were tall, wooden houses built above the water, a bridge connecting the two—something that hadn't been there during his last visit. The water beneath him lapped at the wood, but the structures him were sturdier, and the docks he walked didn't sway like they had long ago. There were signs of damage—wood rotting, scorch marks on the stone—but otherwise, everything was holding together. There were carpenters around Varun replacing and fixing damage made by the water, or by drunken idiots who thought smashing holes into the bridges would take away their anger.

Unfortunately, Brandon had been witness to one too many of those. Usually they were angered by the Hunters, who were disliked and feared. Those drunk enough to wash away their fear, who stood up to the group of men and refused to back down, usually ended up in the small medical centre on the outskirts of the town.

Talk of the next hunt spread throughout the river city, though the excitement came with hope that when the Hunters left, they'd never return. Another reason why Brandon wanted to wait them out; he didn't want them behind him, and much preferred being able to keep his eyes on their backs as they left.

From whispers, he'd learnt there were around twenty of the Hunters in Varun and the surrounding villages, all coming together to hunt in the mountains. Unease kept him quiet and always listening, just in case they were heading in the direction he intended to travel.

Twenty would be hard to fight, especially on his own.

Maybe I should have left when I had the chance, he thought, stopping at the tavern. His room above was scarcely decorated; a cot, washbasin, and a dresser made up the space, and it was small enough to fit him and maybe one other without feeling claustrophobic.

Inside, the air was warmer than it was outside in the sun. Brandon wiped at his brow lazily before stepping up to the bar. The owner barely glanced at him before sliding him a mug of sweet wine. One sip told him it had been watered down, but he didn't drink it for the taste.

He drank it to forget.

~

When night fell, the people of Varun arose.

Maybe it was because they all worked long hours during the day, but once the sun fell and darkness spread over the land, music and laughter filled the taverns. The drunken words of men and women who wished to drown their fears and sorrows in cheap ale filled the air as they tried to find luck with cards or those who sold their bodies, or just wanted a break from their monotonous routine.

Brandon didn't move from his stool until every seat in the tavern was full and the stench of alcohol permeated the air. On either side of him, locals' had conversations about fish or farming, mundane events that were either praised or condemned. One man was happy because he'd caught enough food to feed his family, while another blamed the contrasting weather for his little produce. They talked of God's blessing the town, or maybe magic being their undoing.

Brandon imagined Celia or Eliza sitting with him, how their hearts would ache for the people of Varun. Though by no means were they poor, they still suffered from the arrival of Hunters and growing population. Celia would be casting magic over the crops to help them grow, while Eliza was bound to seek out the Hunters and put an end to their reign of terror.

He smiled to himself and took another sip of his wine. He'd stopped tasting it three cups ago as he tried to forget.

One night, he decided. He would give himself one night.

"What's got you smiling?" the barkeep asked, dark eyes curious as they flickered from Brandon to the mug he wiped down.

The smile slipped from Brandon's face. "Friends. They would certainly enjoy Varun."

Friends you abandoned, a voice in the back of his head reminded him. *Friends you left so you could drink yourself stupid and drown in your own pathetic sorrows.*

Brandon closed his eyes for a moment and took a breath.

"Rowdy ones, are they?" the barkeep asked just as a table erupted in a joyous tune about babes and wives and a blessing from a God.

The commander opened his eyes and shook his head. "Not at all. They'd love the people. They'd want to help."

When Brandon found the barkeep's eyes, there was a strange glisten in them. "How so?" the man asked, voice tight.

Brandon observed him for a moment before releasing a breath. "Let's just say they have particular talents that would be appreciated in Varun—so long as no one knew about them."

Understanding shone in the barkeep's eyes. "We 'aven't had a magic one in here in years."

Brandon wasn't surprised. There was a chance the last time the river city had seen magic was when Amitel had been there, though during their visit, they'd done nothing to help the people—other than removing those who would see the oracle turned over to the wrong people and burn the village because it was in their way.

"I overheard you the other night," the barkeep continued, "when you were talking to the Hunters. Said you were going to visit family."

Brandon tensed, but nodded slowly.

"I didn't believe you then, and I certainly don't, now." The barkeep met Brandon's eyes. "But I do believe you about your friends. Sound like nice ones."

The commander released a breath. He'd been clutching the mug like a lifeline, but he let it go, half-full but no longer appealing. "I'll be heading off then," Brandon murmured, downing the mouthful of wine left in his cup.

The barkeep pressed his lips together and smiled. "Have a nice night."

The crowd of people parted for Brandon, though their attention never strayed to him. Brandon climbed the stairs two at a time, thoughts heavy, though he could barely distinguish one from another. He wanted to blame the drink, but it didn't affect him like it used to—no matter how much he wished it would.

At the landing, he stopped, low voices carrying into the hall. The door closest to him was cracked open to reveal a room similar to his own, yet filled with three bodies—two of which he recognised as the Hunters he'd met days ago—the leader and his guards.

"Is everything ready?" the leader asked.

One of his men grunted. "Everyone is aware of the change in plans."

"Good." Brandon listened as footsteps sounded behind the door, the wooden floorboards creaking with each step, growing closer to where he hid.

Brandon stepped away and wished the shadows would surround him, protect him. He waited for the door to open, to reveal he was listening, but it never happened.

"When will we leave?" someone asked. Brandon assumed it was one of the other men, not the leader.

There was another pause. The leader's voice was soft as he replied, "We start for the valley at dawn."

A frown curved Brandon's lips, but he retreated into the shadows of the stairs, climbing them quickly up to his room. His satchel was already packed, but he added three days' worth of rations he'd been collecting around the village to the mix, making sure to use the jug of clean water to fill his canister.

Dread washed over him as he shouldered the bag and slipped back out into the hall, careful of the cracked door and whoever waited within. The hallway remained clear, and so did the stairs, though at the bottom he ran into a couple too busy removing clothes to care about him.

Outside the tavern, only the remnants of music remained. There were a few men outside drunk enough to brave the cold, but he felt no watchful eyes, saw no shadows moving. There was no magic in the air, no danger that he could sense.

He had perhaps five hours on his side before the Hunters left

Varun in search of their next kill. Brandon berated himself for waiting around, cursed his naivety. Because Riders would seek out safety; they would be attracted to magic, powerful and ancient magic that could protect them from those hunting them.

They would go to the oracle, and not even know what they were stumbling upon.

Brandon let the darkness consume him and disappeared into the night.

10

BEFORE

The door slammed behind Enya, leaving Brandon and Amitel alone with her mercenaries. The first bolt released, singing through the air. Brandon jumped on the closest man, ducking beneath the bow, slipping around his back. Brandon used the man's burly body as a shield, wrapping his arms around his thick neck and tightening his hold, remaining still despite the squirming mercenary in his grip. The man fell limp, and Brandon released him.

The mercenary beside Brandon spun, reloading his crossbow. Amitel, the slippery warlock, was nowhere to be seen. Brandon bit down a growl and rushed the second mercenary, knocking the tall man back into a wooden beam. The building shook with the impact. Brandon ducked a punch and forced the crossbow into his own hands as he slammed his knee into the man's groin. The mercenary dropped with a groan; Brandon loaded a bolt and aimed at a third mercenary, clicking the release and watched as it lodged in his throat.

Brandon ducked behind a wall of crates and closed his eyes for a moment. The fire outside licked at the walls, turning the establishment into a stove. Sweat beaded on his brow, tickling his upper lip. He wiped it away with the sleeve of his shirt and peaked over the crates to take in the room.

There were five mercenaries left, but their weapons lowered, their eyes glowing gold. Their tense bodies shook, lips quivering.

Brandon rose quietly, gaze lifting to the rafters. Hidden in the shadows, Amitel stood like a puppet master, arms spread wide, his long fingers moving like a pianist's. Eyes closed, the magic wrapped over his arms, and into the five beneath him. Intrigued, Brandon left the safety of the crates, wiping his brow as he did, and circled the mercenaries. They were unaware of him, and he couldn't help but wonder how.

It reminded him of a spell Isolde had shown him, only she had done it to the dead.

Within the blink of an eye, the necks of the mercenaries snapped. They dropped with a thud, their weapons clanging, bringing Brandon out of his stupor. He jumped back, gaze dragging up to where Amitel still stood.

And Brandon wasn't sure if he should be impressed, or afraid of what Amitel had just done.

The warlock didn't speak, and instead stepped off the beam, landing with a roll and popping up beside Brandon. Blood trickled from Amitel's nose, but he wiped it away quickly, brushing it off like Brandon hadn't seen what the magic had done to him.

"We need to go after Enya," Amitel said, shaking his head as he started for the door she'd left through. "She couldn't have gone far, and we cannot let her leave with the oracle."

Brandon swallowed hard and looked down at the bodies. The mercenary he'd left alive was gone. But Brandon knelt and picked through their pockets.

"What in the Goddess' name are you doing?" Amitel asked. Brandon didn't look up, and instead continued his search. There were weapons, bags of coins, but nothing indicative of where Enya would be going.

He released a shuddering breath and bowed his head. "We're running out of time anyway," he muttered. "Enya probably has contingency plans and already knows we're coming for her. We need to know where she's going."

Amitel was silent for a moment. Brandon didn't look up as the warlock approached him. "Are you more angry at yourself for leading her to the oracle? Or at the oracle for basically saying Isolde's sacrifice during the resurgence had been for nothing?"

Brandon's eyes snapped up, and he leapt to his feet. He slammed Amitel into a beam, and the building shook again, but the warlock merely smirked. "Don't say her name."

"It's both then. You feel like a failure, and you want nothing more than to go back to sulking over the woman you love." Amitel shoved back, causing Brandon to stumble into the bodies. "Think, Brotherhood. They taught you how to use your brain during training, didn't they? Enya needs to sail south to the Courts. So where would she need to go in order to do that?"

Brandon clenched his jaw. "The southern ferry."

Amitel nodded. "Precisely. Now, if we don't leave, the fire will consume this God's forsaken building, and us with it."

Stalking around him, Brandon headed for the door, and entered the destruction he had wrought.

The fire had taken most of the northern village, but as people escaped, the flames weakened. Other than the crackling of wood and their footsteps, Brandon heard nothing.

They ran to the southern docks, where barges and boats had ferried visitors, fishermen, and those living on the mainland to and from the river-logged village. But like the northern docks, most of the moorings had been destroyed, ships sunk so those from Varun couldn't escape.

There were more bodies floating in the ruins of the burning village, left behind by those who survived. Brandon almost paused by the body of a woman, half claimed by the lapping waves, her arm outstretched to someone who could not save her. Where there should have been fear, there was a sadness left in her unseeing eyes.

Amitel skidded to a halt and held out an arm to stop Brandon. Halfway across the lake, a barge glided to the shore, where a cart drawn by four houses awaited. On the barge was a large crate.

The oracle.

"We're too late," Brandon hissed, stepping away from the edge of the dock. He ran a hand over his hair and turned away from the shore.

"We can still reach her," Amitel said after a long moment. "We just need a boat."

Brandon spun to face the warlock. "Can't you do something?"

"What I did back there with the mercenaries depleted a lot of my magic. Enya's charm and the fire are eating away at my energy."

"Then why did you do it?" Brandon asked, narrowing his eyes. "Why risk it?"

Amitel pressed his lips into a thin line; he stepped away from Brandon as red trickled into the gold of his irises and walked to the edge, rubbing his hands together. "I needed to know if what she said was true," he replied. "I had to make sure that what she was doing was of her own accord, and not some elaborate story she'd woven because there was another calling the shots."

"And?" Brandon stepped up beside him, and though his anger still burned in his veins at what Amitel might have risked, he understood. "Did you get your answer?"

"Yes." He swallowed audibly. "She's lost her mind. Her mercenaries sense it. She is no longer the sane leader they once followed. Something shifted in her, and they fear it."

"Can we use that?"

Amitel met his stare, then let his gaze flicker over Brandon's shoulder. "I believe we can, yes."

Brandon frowned and followed his stare; behind them, the mercenary Brandon had let live pushed a small boat through a sinking portion of the dock. If he had noticed them, he didn't make it obvious.

Turning back to Amitel, Brandon raised a brow. "I suppose one more won't be too hard."

The warlock smirked. He cocked his head and lifted a hand, closing his fingers into a fist. Behind Brandon, a body dropped into the water, and once again, blood trickled from Amitel's nose.

Brandon ignored it and instead started for the boat. "Let's stop her before she can hurt anyone else."

~

The small boat carried them to the shore, despite the rotting oars and debris forcing them far from where the barge had landed. They rowed only by the light of the fire behind them and hoped Enya and her men hadn't seen them cross the lake.

There were no houses lining the shore, instead a row of thick trees and farmland beyond. Brandon and Amitel clung to the shadows of the forest with weapons drawn. There was no doubt Enya had left behind her men to set fire to the coastline to hide their escape. Brandon just hoped they could stop the mercenaries before they carried out her plan.

The smell of smoke wasn't as thick, but it still clung to him. Its rage lessened, but as it consumed the village, Brandon hoped it would die out with the escape of survivors.

But if it reached land... he wasn't sure what would happen.

Laughter cut through the night, a stark change from the gentle song of the lake and the *whoosh* of the fire. Brandon held up a hand, and they stopped behind a thick tree-trunk as three mercenaries carried a barrel into an open field. They spoke Lazirothian, their accents thick. Brandon couldn't understand the words, but Amitel shook his head.

"They're talking about the oracle," he murmured. "They know nothing of Enya's plan. They think they're selling it to a king across the sea. They think they're going to be rich." He paused and frowned. "Enya has a ship docked at the closest port. She plans on burning that, too."

Brandon tensed as the mercenaries stopped and opened the top of the barrel. "We cannot let that happen," he replied. "No one else needs to die."

Stepping away from the tree, Brandon slipped into the space between the two trunks and palmed a dagger. He let his mind clear and aimed at the first man, the one closest to the barrel. Cocking his wrist, Brandon released a breath and threw the dagger. It soared through the air and caught the mercenary in the throat. As the man dropped, Brandon had a second dagger in the air.

The final mercenary shouted and abandoned the barrel, but a third dagger entered Brandon's hand. He cocked his arm and snapped, releasing it once more as the mercenary approached, but the man ducked, stumbling to the ground before gathering himself and rushing towards them.

Brandon reached for another dagger, but the mercenary found him. Brandon ducked a punch and threw out his hand, the heel of his palm hitting the centre of the man's chest. The mercenary grunted, falling back a step, but he growled something in Lazirothian and pulled a sword free.

But he collapsed, the sword dropping with a dull thud. Amitel had slipped behind him with a knife now lodged in the back of the mercenary's neck. A gurgling sound left his lips.

"Thanks," Brandon said, chest heaving. He knelt and picked up the mercenary's sword. It looked as if it had once been decorated with crystals and gems, but had since been picked free. With a shrug, Brandon sheathed it.

Amitel stared at the body, then the barrel. "We'll warn someone of its location. We don't have time to dispose of it."

"Agreed." Brandon stepped over the body. "We should go. We don't know how many more Enya has set up."

Amitel said nothing as they ran for the road; on the horizon, the sky lightened, signalling the dawn of a new day. A soft wind carried ash from the village, dusting the land like snow in winter.

Brandon clenched his jaw and pushed himself. Amitel kept pace beside him until they were on the road. From their position, he could see the docks and the barge, but no cart and horses. Ruts cut through the ash, leading through the hills.

They shared a look and started down the road; sweat lined Brandon's upper lip as they ran, but he didn't wipe it away, instead focusing on his breathing, on the smoke that tinged the air and clung to the inside of his mouth. He focused on the loud thud of his heart rather than *her* name rolling off of Amitel's tongue like a curse.

Voices around the next bend made Brandon slow to a stop. He wasn't sure how many men were left with Enya, if she had a small army with her, or only a few to guard the oracle.

As if sensing his thoughts, Amitel shook his head and pointed to his ear. He circled the lobe with his pointer finger twice and closed his eyes.

Brandon had learnt the trick from Celia during their time with the Cadiran army, when they had not been allowed to partake in meetings with Isolde and the generals.

Amitel's eyes snapped open. "She's alone."

"What?" Brandon edged closer to the voice, and realised he heard only one: hers, though she sounded different as she spoke to the oracle. "Why?"

Amitel shook his head. "They abandoned her."

11

THE LAST ONES

The ferry ran all hours of the day, and even into the night. The old man captaining it said nothing as Brandon boarded the small vessel, leaving the lights and drunken songs of Varun behind.

Across the lake, a small road snaked into the mountains, dark and shadowed, partially illuminated by a few small huts gathered on either side of the road. They lined the lake and the shallow strip of dock that separated the land from the water.

When the ferry idled to a stop, Brandon paid the ferryman two silver pieces, pulled his cloak over his head, and began his trek past the few houses still awake so late.

Lanterns set against front doors rattled as he passed, open shutters revealing warm homes within. Brandon paused in front of a squat cottage, the exterior a blend of stone and wood. The open window revealed a small room filled with paintings and tiny figurines. Tucked into a bed, a child stared up at a weathered woman.

"In the days of old, there used to be great and powerful beasts that roamed this land. They took to the skies and to the seas, slept beneath mountains and traversed the land we now call home." The old woman patted the bed, a wistful look entering her dark, tired eyes. "They called them dragons, and their riders, Drakons, for they shared the blood of the beasts and that gave them the magic to communicate and share a bond unlike anything seen in these lands."

"Ma, be careful," another woman hissed. Younger. Brandon spied her in the corner of the room; she was a spitting image of the older woman, though fewer lines framed her eyes and lips. Unlike the weathered woman, there was a spark of terror in her dark eyes, like she expected the Dragon Hunters to break down their door.

The old woman made a sound and continued, "They were dragons, and they once ruled our land. They fought in our wars, protected our people, spoke to the gods. They *were* gods, to those who were not given the gift to ride them."

The young woman said something else, and they fell silent. Brandon closed his eyes and rubbed them tiredly. The Hunters had the people of Varun in a death grip, forcing terror into the hearts of those who likely grew up hearing stories of the legendary Riders.

Now, they feared even speaking their names would bring retribution.

Before he could move on, the old woman said, "They still live with us, you know. We call them the last ones." The small child made a squeaking sound. "They sleep and wait until the last great clan of Drakon's can return and take their place at the head of the next rise."

Brandon pressed his lips into a firm line as he started for the mountains. The words of the old woman tightened something in his gut.

The last great clan, she'd said. So flippantly, he wondered if it, too, was just an old tale spun by men and women who never saw even the hints of the great creatures they spoke of, or if there was some truth behind it, like a warning.

~

The long days burned, but Brandon continued his hike until the familiar pocket of land—a valley deep in the hills of Laziroth, hidden further inland—came into view. Trees hid the land, but he knew what lay beneath: ruins of an old God, and somewhere within the mountains, the oracle.

Brandon braced himself at the tree line for a moment before leaving the path. He pulled at memories from his time with Amitel, when they had hunted the oracle for a man who would have paid handsomely for her. Now, those memories felt like they stemmed from someone else entirely. He did not recognise the man he'd been.

It'd been weeks since Isolde's death. He and Celia, along with the Brotherhood and Blood Witches who had sided with the Ecix, had returned to the Labyrinth mountains. Despite winning the war, they still failed.

He remembered the calm fury of the High Council when they'd been presented with Isolde's corpse. She needed to be returned to the Temple of the Ecix, where she would be laid to rest and returned to the aether so that she could return, eventually, as another.

That day had forged him a new path, and it had been the day he'd left everything he'd known behind.

If he had been anyone else, he would have been killed for wanting to leave the Brotherhood. The immortality would have been taken from him, and any magic that had kept him alive during the war would have been reversed. He would have died from the wounds he'd received like any other mortal, would have aged like a mortal within moments.

He would have joined Isolde, perhaps.

His heart stuttered in his chest as he continued the hike into the valley. He'd considered dying that day, hoped that maybe his Brother's would set him free, but it had been part of his punishment—his immortality. And during the years that followed, he believed he deserved it.

The forest remained quiet as he walked. He had no idea how far behind him the Hunters were, if they'd left any sooner than they'd planned.

Now, in the forest leading into the valley, Brandon wasn't sure if he'd make it.

Hunters were faster, stronger than regular mortals. They lived perhaps only several years more, and their strength could rival that of a Knight of the Brotherhood. Brandon had to reach the oracle first—he knew he couldn't take them in a fight. He knew the Riders hiding in the valley couldn't, either—that was, if they were there like the hunters believed.

Perhaps the Hunters had been spinning stories like the old woman, forcing Brandon out of Varun. Perhaps they knew of what he sought and tricked him into leaving for the valley. Had he not learnt his lesson two hundred years before?

Brandon paused and closed his eyes, locking away those burning memories.

He spent hours locked in his thoughts, unable to dwell on anything for too long.

When the valley finally appeared between the thick tree trunks, he stopped, listening for the familiar hum of life.

But there was nothing, save for the rustle of branches and leaves.

A shudder ran down his spine. If the magic was still there, he couldn't feel it. And that terrified him.

An hour crawled by, and he counted each step so his mind wouldn't wander.

There was no doubt, however, that he was being followed.

Brandon didn't stop, not as the valley grew closer. The keen senses of the Brotherhood helped him as he navigated the thick bush, where the light couldn't break through the heavy foliage above his head. The smell of rain tickled his nose, the soil beneath his boots wet. He doubled back every so often to cover his tracks.

The sun lowered in the sky. In a matter of a few hours, he'd be completely cloaked in darkness. It would make for easier travel, but it would also leave him open to any sort of attack, either from the Hunters or the one who followed him.

A trickle of magic crawled down his spine and danced with the Blood Magic in his veins.

It wasn't the Hunters; the magic that coursed through them was different, a gradual build of power that came from many sources and their own need to hone it.

If Amitel or Celia were with him, they might have been able to understand it. They might have been able to help.

For a moment, Brandon let himself fall into the pit of what might be. He knew he should have sent word to them by now; days at sea, then days spent trapped in Varun had given him plenty of time to reach out, check on Eliza... but he'd been afraid. Afraid of how she might react, or what she might say. He could have at least written to Celia, but he feared that she, too, still wasn't pleased with him.

Was Eliza already married to the prince? Had the Blood Witches whisked away by so that she might finally ascend?

Brandon stopped and sucked in a breath. Time felt different in Laziroth, like he had been gone only days, but he knew weeks had passed. The long days at sea had turned into long nights in the river city. He'd been gone at least two weeks—in that time, had everything changed for Eliza? Or was the clock ticking closer to her freedom being taken from her?

Maybe I should have brought her with me. The thought struck him hard, forcing him to lean against a nearby tree. His chest heaved as he wondered what might have been different had he gone to Eliza the night of her ball and whisked her away.

She would have loved leaving Cadira, but the cost?

He wasn't sure if she would risk her family to escape the confines of the palace, of the crown.

A shard of light struck through a break in the canopy of leaves above him, illuminating something further down the hill. A large mound, hidden in the greenery.

Brandon squinted at the structure hidden beneath a layer of moss and vines. He hadn't seen it the last time he'd walked into the valley; he turned in a slow circle to take in his surroundings, but the path had changed over time.

He started for the structure, side stepping upturned roots and logs. He heard Eliza's voice in the back of his mind, telling him to investigate further. The closer he got, the larger it became; taller than him, it looked as though it could have been a moss covered rock, maybe the skeleton of a hut, abandoned to time, returned to the wildness of the jungle.

But something about it tickled a memory in the back of his mind. There was magic hidden within. It crawled over his skin in warning, causing the hairs on his arms to stand on end.

He stopped and stared up at the structure; it towered over him, the moss so thick it blanketed the exterior. The magic was heavier, clinging to something ancient. Perhaps he should have walked away, left its secrets alone. But curiosity won out, and he reached for the moss and started pulling it and the vines aside.

The first scrape of his nails against the outside of the structure made him pause. The moss came off in clumps in his hands, and when he dropped it, he spied what looked like wood, but it was hard, damaged. He felt the tip of what might have been a blade, but as he ran his calloused fingers over the point, he realised the shape resembled that of a spike, jutting down from the roof of a cave opening.

It was the only large obstacle in the area, though, with no other rock formation around it. He now stood on the side of the mountain, so it was possible it was a cave, he thought.

Brandon's heart thundered. Did he have time to investigate? He bit his lip, taking a step away.

The magic meant something. And he needed to know what.

The moss fell away, revealing what looked like bone. *No,* he thought, brushing more away from the point, *a tooth.* Palming a dagger, he used it as a knife to cut away vines. Around him they fell like ropes used to tie down a beast, snapping away to uncover something long dead.

Brandon took a step back and blinked once, twice, at what he'd uncovered.

The skull of a dragon.

He could see the outline now; the long nose and nostrils, the indentations of eye sockets, rows of sharp teeth that would have once been salvaged and used to create the weapons of Riders.

It was only the skull, and yet he felt like he'd found the entire beast, asleep within the mountain, just waiting for the right person to wake it.

The shard of light, though growing dim, glinted off something in the dragon's mouth. Brandon narrowed his eyes and stooped, pulling his sword free as he did.

Using the tip of the blade, he poked it between the teeth of the dragon. It dragged against what sounded like metal; it tinged unnaturally in the old forest, louder than he'd expected. Drawing his weapon back, Brandon sheathed his sword and frowned.

His heart thundered against his ribcage. Slowly, he drew closer, acutely aware of the world around him; the birds who did not sing, the buzz of insects hidden in the bark of the surrounding trees, the sweat beading on the back of his neck, and the missing shadow, who he hoped had left before he'd found the last remnants of a once legendary society.

Brandon reached into the mouth of the dragon for the metal; the tips of his fingers skimmed the rings of a thin chain, but before he could grasp it, it fell out of reach.

He swore under his breath and snatched his hand back. Standing, he circled the skull, moving to stand directly in front of it. When he cut at the vines, he realised the front teeth were missing from the top and bottom jaw, leaving a small opening into the beast's mouth.

A twig snapped somewhere behind him; Brandon spun, dagger in hand, and searched the darkness of the forest. His shadow had returned, or someone else had found him.

I should leave, he thought, yet his feet remained planted in front of the skull. If he left without uncovering the dragon's secrets, he was certain someone else would, and he knew in his gut he couldn't let that happen.

Brandon's shoulders tensed as he ducked, entering the mouth of the dragon. He smiled to himself, but it fell away a moment later as his eyes adjusted to the darkness. Lying in a patch of moss was the skeletal remains of a rider. The leathers were still intact, the skull of the rider protected by its helm.

The commander shivered, eyes grazing over the body. He'd been close to touching the head from where he'd reached in. He'd likely been touching the helm, which was a dim metal split in half and damaged. It was the only item that suggested he had once been a warrior, any weapon long since gone, or buried by vegetation.

Brandon shook his head and stepped towards the opening once more. A twinge of disappointment made him stop and turn back. He spied something in the moss.

Outside the skull, another twig snapped. Brandon snatched up the item and climbed out of the dragon's mouth.

Eyes burned the back of his skull. The shadow had certainly returned, but they didn't attack. He shoved the item into his pocket and continued his trek down the mountain.

12

THE RUINS

The forest reclaimed the ruins of the once beautiful temple grounds. Two hundred years and the only remnants of Brandon's memories lay in the stonework beneath his feet, cracked and crumbling, claimed by crawling roots and thick moss, the debris of tree litter and a patchwork of stone and brush.

Where there had once been an opening that led into the oracles den, a tree stood—so tall Brandon had to crane his neck up to look at it. He shielded his eyes as he took in the long branches that created a twisted roof above his head, strange symbols etched into the trunk and at the bases of thick branches. He frowned, studying one of the symbols closest to him.

It was one he didn't recognise, a strange knot with what might have been an image of fire in the middle. He touched a thumb to the etching, grazed over the edges. It didn't feel new, not rough like someone had recently made the carvings. It was smooth, growing with the tree.

Brandon remembered when Amitel planted it, accelerated its growth. It blocked the path to the oracle and magicked the doorway to another location. Hidden to all—except Amitel.

Clenching his jaw, Brandon stepped away and tried to ignore

the pounding in his ears at the thought of the warlock. Two hundred years ago, the site had been harder to access. Perhaps since their last visit, the once ancient magic had slowly disappeared, leaving behind what it once hid. Something had been in place to keep the oracle away from those who wished to use her.

Had they broken that seal and lost her? Brandon shook his head. Amitel had done well to relocate the entrance to her den and had done what he could to protect her.

Or so Brandon hoped...

What he didn't want to think of was Amitel betraying this secret to the Dark Master. It hadn't crossed his mind earlier that perhaps his entire trek to the valley had been in vain. What if the Dark Master had already been there, taken the chained girl and swept her away to wherever he hid?

Brandon closed his eyes and sucked in a breath. The questions would do him no good. According to Amitel, not even he knew where the oracle was. He would have had to physically be in the valley to find her once more. Otherwise, one would have to find her by chance.

"It doesn't mean the Dark Master didn't find her on his own— or Amitel didn't come back and take her," he muttered aloud as he searched his surroundings once more.

Half way down the mountain, his shadow had disappeared. It hadn't stopped Brandon from checking over his shoulder every couple of feet, like the shadow would reappear with a knife in hand.

Brandon sighed and rubbed his eyes. The sun was low, well below the trees. A cool breeze rustled the leaves around him. Stepping away from the tree, Brandon touched the chain in his pocket.

As soon as I set up camp, I'll look at it, he decided. He would need to find somewhere safe before the sun completely set. The valley was too open, compromised by the ruins of the temple. Though nature gradually retook the land once dedicated to the old magic of Laziroth, it did not mean he was safe in its gentle hands.

From memory, there was a bay of large boulders not far from the entrance, up the side of the mountain. Brandon started in the direction of the outcropping, his mind straying to the last time he'd been there. He wondered if the bodies were still hidden where he and Amitel had placed them when they'd gone after the mercenaries who had stolen the oracle away to Varun.

Brandon walked for what felt like an hour, and released a heavy breath when the rocks appeared. They were aged like the rest of the valley, reminding him of the dragon skull, but they were large enough to give him shelter—and cover against prying eyes.

Hidden in the gathered debris of the forest, a bleached skull stared up at him. Brandon pressed his lips into a grimace. Were the spirits of the men he killed lingering in the valley? He was glad he couldn't see the dead like Eliza could.

He didn't bother to check if any other bones remained at the stones. They'd been weighed down by armour, but that wouldn't have stopped scavengers from feasting on them.

Though the days were warm, he couldn't ignore the chill seeping beneath his skin. A fire would have been nice; just the semblance of warmth would have done wonders, and yet he hesitated. A fire would alert anyone nearby that he was there. He'd been lucky so far not to have the Hunters catch his scent. The last thing he needed was to risk his safety to warm his sore hands.

Instead, he went in search of anything edible. He would take nuts and mushrooms if it meant not having to eat the stale bread left in his pack.

Though the forest offered little—at least in Cadira he could have whispered a request to the pixies, who would have brought him berries and apples—he found the heads of small vegetables hidden below the rock outcrop. He grimaced. They were edible, though likely would have tasted better boiled over a fire with butter.

Cadira crossed his mind, his time spent travelling the lands. He had spent years within the Willican Forest with the pixies and the creatures once only native to the Fae lands. They had, like mortals and the Half-Fae, travelled far. But the little folk no longer roamed Laziroth, scared off when the Hunters rose to power.

But thoughts of Cadira, of his time in the Willican, dredged up memories of his life after Isolde. His heart ached, but he forced it down, slipping those memories back into the darkness of his mind. He returned his focus to the valley and found food, but the smell of soot filled Brandon's nose as he stepped into a ring of blackened earth.

He knelt and touched the pile. His fingers came back coated in dark ash. Someone had recently been in the valley, not far from the tree. Every part of him tensed as he stood and searched the surrounding brush. Thick tree trunks coated in moss, vines that swung in a soft breeze. An insect buzzed nearby.

But there was no one around.

It didn't mean he wasn't alone, though.

13

WARNINGS OF WAR

Brandon couldn't help but bask in the dawn glow that surrounded her. It blanketed her bare shoulders, submerging her olive skin in a golden light, highlighting the smooth peaks of her breasts and the length of her legs as she stretched them out in front of her.

A small smile played at his lips as he took in his beloved. The tip of her chin as she lifted her face to the sun, her closed eyes, the subtle curve of her lips, like she knew he was watching.

The reality, the memories of her dead body cradled in Celia's arms, the mess of his departure from the Brotherhood, seeing Eliza for the first time—the spitting image of his Isolde—came crashing down around him.

Brandon closed his eyes against the memories, wishing them away, even for a couple more moments. He wanted to take her in, wanted to be in her presence, just for a few moments longer, without being assaulted with the truth.

She was dead, visiting him in a memory.

It was the first time they'd been together, the memory she'd chosen. Or maybe he had. It sometimes crept into his mind; the banks of Lake Mab, their small camp, the stars and moons of

Cadira watching over them as they made love.

When he opened his eyes again, he found Isolde watching him, his shirt draped over her frame. She gave him a feline-like smile. "Hello, my love."

Her voice sent shivers down his spine. "I cannot believe this isn't real," Brandon murmured. He was too afraid to approach the blanket, despite how much he wanted to take her in his arms. The need burned within him, a feeling he only thought would exist in the darkness of his thoughts, in the back of memories he tried to keep hidden away.

Her smile turned soft as she rose. Isolde crossed the small space between them, her feet barely touching the forest floor. "I am here, just enough." She reached a hand up to cup his cheek; the feel of her skin almost broke him.

When she pressed her lips against his, for a moment, his senses went wild; she smelt like the lemon and lavender soap she always used, her lips so soft they felt like clouds. She cupped his cheeks, he felt the callouses on her palms from their nightly sword fighting lessons, but her touch was gentle, real.

Brandon forgot everything except her. Deepening the kiss, he wrapped his arms around her middle and picked her up. She made a sound in the back of her throat as her hands ran down his neck to the back of his head, where she laced her fingers through his hair.

He lowered her carefully onto the blanket and hovered over her with one knee wedged between her thighs. He cupped the back of her neck as his other hand trailed the length of her body to the bare skin of her thigh where his shirt rose to pool around her abdomen. Heat built within him as he cupped her thigh and moved his hand beneath the shirt. A small gasp escaped Isolde's lips.

He could stay there, caught in her embrace, locked in the memories that once threatened to drown him.

Isolde pulled back and blinked up at him. "I never thought I would touch you again," she whispered, hand hovering over his cheek, "but this must be all."

Brandon frowned, blinking as she and the lake fell away. The darkness shifted, and he found himself standing in a dark room. Isolde stood across from him, her arms crossed tightly over her chest. She pursed her lips and refused to meet his gaze, instead curling in on herself, like she planned to disappear.

He wanted to go to her, and yet he was trapped, feet glued to the ground. "Isolde."

She didn't look up. "I came here to warn you."

His heart stuttered as he took in her shuddering frame; the longer she remained in the darkness, the smaller she became. The shadows threatened to claim her, and he could do nothing to save her.

Brandon clenched his jaw. His heart yearned for her, but his memories screamed at him to think, to remember what had happened the last time he'd lost her.

But his heart won. "Please." He reached for her, but she shook her head.

"A war is coming." Isolde curled her hands into fists; her posture changed, and she unfurled, pacing the darkness with frenzied steps. "I knew what you sought would be impossible to find, and now it will all come to an end."

Brandon froze. "What do you mean?"

"It will be greater than the Resurgence." She looked up, pausing her pacing. "And it will surpass the Great War."

"What happened?" he asked. "What happened to Eliza? Celia?"

Isolde took a step back. "He knows the truth."

Brandon blinked, and she was gone, leaving him in the dark room alone.

"Isolde!"

Brandon woke, sweat beading on his brow, heart thundering in his chest. Every breath he took burned; his ribs ached like he'd broken several of them, his muscles stiff and worn. He winced as he rose, pain pounding in his skull.

As he rubbed at his eyes, he remembered Isolde, her shrinking figure succumbing to the darkness. The fear thick in her voice, her warning burning in his heart.

The forest was quiet, the valley below him still. The sun broke through the canopy of leaves and warmed his camp. It sat high in the sky; not quite mid-day, but still late enough that he swore under his breath.

Brandon cursed himself, not only for sleeping so long, but for what happened with Isolde. Everything in him told him she was right, and yet he wanted to believe that everything in Cadira was fine. That in his absence, something terrible hadn't happened to Eliza.

His need to find the oracle grew deeper and more frenzied as Isolde's warning replayed in his ears. Brandon ate quickly despite his stomach's protests and gathered his satchel and weapons. He felt no eyes on him as he went about his business, but the valley was large, its surroundings dense, so he remained vigilant. He might not sense the eyes now, but he knew there was a chance they were still out there.

The valley opened up around him; what he might have mistaken as a fallen tree had the distinct markings of a column, curved at either end, snapped in the middle. He couldn't remember if it had been standing the last time he and Amitel had been there. Two more lay covered in moss and the debris of the forest. He passed them, clenching his jaw.

A path cut through the ruins, and he followed it, hand hovering over the pommel of his sword. Aside from the great tree standing in the place of the gateway, there was no sign of an entrance into the den.

Brandon marked the outer edges of the old temple, listened for the hum of Amitel's magic; he'd learnt over the years how to recognise the faint trace of power, the unique signature that belonged only to Amitel. Every magic wielder had their own.

When he couldn't sense it around the ruins, Brandon set off further into the valley, where dense foliage protected the old temple from prying eyes. From a distance, the brush looked impenetrable, an emerald wall around the site. But as he trekked through the moss-covered stone that lay around him like graves, he found small paths woven through the shadows.

He paused as a shiver danced over his skin. Magic called for what lived in his veins, but it wasn't Amitel's familiar signature.

Brandon watched as ash appeared before his eyes, forming a burning piece of parchment that dropped into his waiting hands.

He held his breath as he read.

Thorne, it's Eliza.

Something happened. Not bad, but... actually, it was really bad.

Do you remember how Xeb and Alastor mentioned Azula's dagger? Well, Celia and I thought we could find it, that maybe we'd be able to summon it. With Amitel's help, we left the palace and took Alicsar with us—bad idea, we know.

We went back to Azula's city below the Spring Manor. We didn't find much, but Celia went to another location—a temple in the Willican Forest. It used to be one dedicated to Azula. Celia found a map that would take us to the dagger.

We went into the Fae Territory—and before you write back to yell at me and tell me how dumb that was, don't worry. We had two of the Brotherhood and a Faery with us, so we were fine.

Anyway, we almost got it. I almost had the dagger, Thorne. I was this close, and I lost it. Apparently, I wasn't ready.

I wish you were here to tell me what to do. I mean, just a little. I wish I knew what you were thinking.

We could have used you out there.

I hope you find whatever it is you're looking for. I will marry Alicsar in a week.

Write back, you asshole. I need to know you're still alive.

-Eliza

A smile threatened to break out on Brandon's face as he read the letter again. He'd done well in forcing himself to lock away thoughts of Eliza, and yet one simple letter threatened to undo all of it. Because he missed her.

Although he didn't appreciate being called an asshole.

His jaw clenched, and he shook his head. He supposed he deserved it after what he'd put her through.

Brandon released the letter and watched as it returned to ash. Fear spiked inside him for what had happened, but he could not stop now, not when he was so close. Not when he could fix it, fix everything.

Isolde had been right. But Eliza needed the dagger. She needed to have some kind of control.

He understood that.
It meant he needed to find the oracle more than ever.
He just hoped the answers would be with the ancient being.

14

THE SOULS OF DRAGONS

The snap of a twig forced Brandon out of his thoughts about Eliza and the dagger, and his need for the oracle. He unsheathed his sword and let it hang loosely from his fingertips. Something rustled in the brush before him, leading further into the valley.

Brandon rolled his shoulders back and followed the sound. It was either a small animal or his shadow. Either way, he planned on learning the truth.

Brandon traced the sound to a larger path in the underbrush. It was small and could have been made by animals, but hidden in a muddy patch beneath heavy green leaves, he spied a human sized footprint. A frown crossed his lips. But he followed the direction of the print, staying low. There were no whispers from the forest, though magic danced over his skin, unfamiliar and feather-light, he almost brushed it aside.

The path came to an end at the edge of a thick line of trees; the trunks were wide, closer together, almost like a wall. It reminded him of the pixie circles he would find in Cadira. A pang of worry shot through him, making him pause.

Eliza played at the back of his mind, her letter burnt into his thoughts. He had no choice but to return to her with more than empty promises.

He had to give her a reason to survive.

Brandon circled the grove, searching for an entrance; a large enough gap between the trees to squeeze through, or a gateway. The magic was heavier, like a film over his skin, but it did not fight him.

Like called to like, despite being so different.

Thin branches braided like a lattice wound through the thick trunks of trees. Small flowers, white and pale yellow, bloomed from almost hidden buds, a sweet scent tickling his nose. Bees flitted from flower to flower, their buzz soft as they worked.

An archway caught his eye, and he paused. A curtain of vines covered a dark entrance, one he almost missed, but as he stepped closer, the welcoming magic of the grove settled on his skin, a whisper of pixies dancing on the breeze ruffling his hair.

Brandon tightened his grip on his sword and pulled back the vines. He expected to find someone protecting the entrance, but those who knew anything about the old pixie magic knew the groves were shielded against ill intent and dark magic.

Whoever was within likely expected the knowledge of the grove to be forgotten by those of Lazirothian descent.

But Brandon knew better than most about the magic.

He couldn't help but wonder why he and Amitel hadn't found the grove during their first trip to the oracle. It would have certainly served as a safe location against the mercenaries. As the thought crossed his mind, Brandon winced, remembering that two hundred years ago, he had not been the saviour he so wished he was; he'd been the ill intent, shadowed by his grief and anger.

Hesitation crept into his mind. He considered what might happen if he stepped foot within, what might happen to whoever hid behind the wall of ancient magic. Would his appearance be dangerous for them—or for himself?

Brandon released a heavy breath and steeled himself.

He stepped beneath the arch and followed a short, dark tunnel into the grove. Another curtain of vines opened onto a large space, not unlike the groves he'd hidden in within the Willican forest. A pond fed by a trickling creek sat to his right, huts surrounding its bank. The earth was bare, muddy, worn down by many feet, the grass sparse. There were three fire pits, two giving off a comfortable warmth as they cooked what smelt like quail over the flames.

Brandon stopped and stared at the small group of twenty or so people; elders and children alike spread throughout the temporary camp built into the hollows of old trees, surrounding one of the fire pits. Carved into the trees were symbols similar to the ones he'd found carved into Amitel's barrier. When he touched the one closest to him, Brandon felt the small tinge of magic at work.

He assessed the group, noting the few tired elders, the younglings hidden by the pond's edge. There were some who looked in their thirties, their bodies honed to fight, to hide. If they attacked, Brandon knew they were the first he would need to take out if he wanted to survive.

The first person to notice him was an older woman; her onyx hair wound atop her head in a crown, braided and thick, streaks of silver shining through the black. She dropped a woven basket and palmed a bone dagger, her hands steady as she stepped forward. "Who are you?"

Brandon recognised the type of weapon; they were rare, forged only by few.

A dragon bone.

Was he so fortunate to have found a clan of Dragon Riders?

Slowly, he sheathed his sword. Others entered what he assumed was the common area, a shared space they all used. Men and women alike pulled weapons of bone, beautiful daggers and swords he'd only ever seen kept in cases at the Brotherhoods compound—or at the hips of Hunters.

"I am not your enemy," he said, raising his hands in surrender. "I'm an ally."

Brandon's gaze flickered between the growing group as he tried to distinguish who was leading the clan. He couldn't help but think of the old woman in Varun and her story of the *Drakon*. Her words were etched into his mind like a song he couldn't forget.

After several moments, a man stepped forward; he was likely in his fifties, with shoulder length ebony hair and keen eyes, skin unblemished by age. He approached Brandon with his hands behind his back, boots silent on the packed earth.

"I sense magic around you," he said, dark eyes grazing over Brandon. "Who are you? You are not one of them."

Them. Brandon knew who the man spoke of. Dropping his hands, Brandon bowed his head in respect. "I am of the Brotherhood. A confidant of the Ecix."

The man's eyes brightened with curiosity. "What does a knight of the legendary Brotherhood want with us?"

Brandon shook his head. "Nothing. It is not you who I seek."

The man narrowed his eyes. "Then what?" he asked.

Brandon's thoughts strayed to his dream, the warning. "I am not here to fight you. I am here because I believe we may be able to help one another."

The leader narrowed his eyes. "How so?"

"I have information that will aid you," Brandon said, looking between the leader and the gathered people. "But I also require your help in return."

The silence around them thickened. Brandon tensed, hands forming fists, as the man stepped back. "I am Khan, leader of the Daggon clan."

Relief washed over Brandon. "Commander Brandon Thorne."

The older man smiled. "We have much to discuss then."

Khan guided Brandon into the camp, past the firepits and the cooking meat, around the pond and past the small huts that lined it. Eyes followed them, but Brandon kept his shoulders back and head high as they entered another section of the grove.

Grass grew in thick layers the further they walked, muffling their footsteps as they approached a secluded building. It was older than the makeshift structures closest to the entrance, the wood darker, damp and heavy with the vines and moss that threatened to reclaim it.

Khan stopped at the entrance, and motioned for Brandon to enter. "Please," the older man said, "let us sit. Have some tea."

Brandon hesitated, his hand almost straying to his sword. He'd trusted the Dragon Rider too quickly, but nothing Khan had said or done had Brandon considering the rider was distrustful. And yet, he'd followed the man into the grotto, where they could kill him in the blink of an eye.

After a moment, Brandon relented and ducked to enter the hut. Inside, the walls were bare, the back smooth stone. A woven rug covered the ground, with scattered pillows on either side of a low table.

Khan gestured for Brandon to sit. "We do not have visitors here," he explained, sitting with his legs crossed. "The old magic protects us."

Brandon nodded. "I understand." He unclipped his sword and rested it against the wall before sitting. As he did, Khan poured two cups of steaming tea; the smell of ginger and unusual spices filled the hut, tickling at something in the back of Brandon's nose. He waited for Khan to take a sip first before picking up the cup. The exterior was smooth, almost like wood, but lighter. It was made of bone.

"Why did you come here, Brandon Thorne?"

"Dragon Hunters from Varun are coming," Brandon replied, taking a hesitant sip. The heat burned his tongue, but the taste was pleasant. He put down the cup as the warmth of the hut crawled over his skin. "They were several hours behind me."

Khan frowned and set down his own cup. His gaze flickered from Brandon and down to his hands. A look of fear and uncertainty flashed across his sharp features. "I see."

"You should gather your people and prepare to leave. They know you're here. It's only a matter of time until they locate the grove." Brandon hesitated before adding, "I can help." Eliza crossed his mind as the words left his lips, and although he somewhat regretted his offer, he considered what she would do in his place.

She would have helped. And so would he.

Khan nodded, releasing a breath. "Thank you for alerting us," he replied finally. "We've been here for months. Perhaps we should have moved on sooner. Our ancestors used this grove as a safe place a century ago, and it has served us well." Dark eyes met Brandon's, fear darkening the umber of his irises. "But that is not the only reason why you are here? Not many venture into the valley. Most believe it is cursed."

Brandon ignored the comment and pulled a hand through his hair. "I am searching for something," Brandon started, but he stopped himself from explaining further. Khan might know of the oracle, might sense the old magic still weaving through the valley. And yet Brandon hesitated. "I actually have something for you."

Slowly, he pulled the chain from his pocket. He hadn't had time to look at it properly; sleep had claimed him too quickly the night before, and he'd forgotten about it in his rushed search for the oracle.

Brandon held it out and finally noticed the charm; it reminded him vaguely of the stone Captain Piper had given him, but instead of being the colour of a sunset, it was silver, like opal. When the light caught it, a rainbow of colour ignited on the surface.

Khan took the pendant and cupped it in his hands. "This is the scale of a dragon." He looked up and met Brandon's stare. "How did you come across this?"

"I found it in the mouth of a dragon skull."

Khan raised a brow. "Was the rider with it?" Hope tinged his voice.

Brandon nodded, relief sweeping through him as Khan stared at the scale. "Yes. The forest was hiding it. I only had a moment and took it without understanding what it meant."

"You have no idea how precious this is," he murmured, wrapping his fingers around it tightly. A moment later, he handed it back, sadness filling his eyes.

Frowning, Brandon took the pendant and stared down at it. "What is it, exactly?" he asked, running a finger over the smooth surface.

"A dragon's soul," Khan replied wistfully. "When a dragon is near death, the rider uses their own body and soul to protect the dragon. It became common practice with living dragons when the Hunters rose. My ancestors infused old magic into these pendants. The scale is of the dragon whose spirit resides within."

Brandon had never heard of such practices. He thought back to being a child and finding the remains of the dragon in the sea cave, how it had disappeared almost as quickly. He'd assumed warlocks had been behind it—Amitel had told him once about how warlocks used the magic of bones, like the Blood Witches did blood, to syphon magic—but had there been another reason for the disappearance?

Had there been a pendant with the skull that he hadn't seen?

Brandon looked up from the silver scale and met Khan's eye. "How many dragons do you have with your riders?"

"None." A sadness entered his dark eyes. "We have been

separated from our dragons for centuries. They are hidden throughout the land, in states such as this, waiting to be woken. I have not seen one in my long life, and neither have my people."

Disappointment tightened around Brandon's heart. "How can they be woken?" Brandon dropped the pendant onto the table between them. "How do we bring them back?"

Khan frowned. "Why do you ask?"

"Because there is a war coming. One that will be greater than even the Great War and the Ecix needs you and the riders," he replied, leaning forward.

"The Ecix? I have heard only stories—many dreadful—about that power." Khan shook his head. "I don't think—"

"She isn't a monster." Brandon released a heavy breath, hesitating. "She is a girl who only wants to break the cycle of terror raining down on our lands." And he needs to find a way to help her if he cannot find the oracle. If a war was truly coming, like Isolde warned, then the Dark Master was already prepared.

"And does she know you are here?" Khan asked.

Brandon shook his head. "No. I left to protect her. I left to find a way to help her. And I might know how, but if I can help build an army against the Dark Master, then I will do that."

Khan watched him for a moment. "You would follow her into war?"

"I would do anything for her."

For a moment, Khan regarded him with sad yet curious eyes. It would have made Brandon uncomfortable, but he'd learnt at a young age to bear it. Instead of flinching away, he held the leader's gaze.

"You are either a fool or terribly loyal."

"Perhaps both." Brandon shrugged, a small smile playing at his lips as he reached for the tea. It had cooled just enough not to burn down his throat when he took a long sip. "How do we wake the dragons? If they can be moved to Cadira, they can be protected."

"Powerful necromancy. They are all dead. Their souls are protected, but they need to be unearthed. Their bones, for example." Khan motioned to the tea set, to the weapons decorating his body, even small elements around the hut like needles and hair clips, all beautifully crafted, none of which revealed the truth of their making. "We collect and hold on to even the smallest part of them, so that maybe their souls can reunite with their mortal vessel." Khan hesitated a moment, gaze flickering to the scale. "This does not work sometimes. The magic is... tricky. The scales are imbued with a special magic to make the reconnection easier, stronger."

"Do you have many?" Brandon asked, motioning to the pendant. "Scales, I mean?"

Khan shook his head. "No. Most burial sites were pillaged before the remaining clans could locate them. If there are scales like this out there, they've been taken and destroyed by Hunters."

Brandon stared down at the cup for a moment. He had never heard of the Ecix doing something such as raising an army of dragons. Mortals, yes. He knew Isolde had done so before her death and knew Eliza had learnt how to control the Shadow Soldiers long enough to cut their connection to the Dark Master. But dragons? "Could the Ecix do this?" he asked quietly, uncertain. "Do you think she could raise the dragons?"

Khan hesitated, then shook his head. "I do not know. I know only the stories. There are other things she would need, things I do not know if we have."

Brandon stiffened, then shook his head. "Then search for it," he said. He would not give up, for her sake. "The Ecix will do what she can for you and your people."

The words tumbled from his lips. Making promises such as that should have made him hesitate, yet he could hear her voice in the back of his head. She would be promising the same thing, that he was certain.

"Are you sure?" Khan asked, brows drawn.

"Yes. Give her a chance."

Khan blinked once, then shook his head. He shielded his emotions as he took another sip of tea. "We have been escaping persecution for centuries. We have been hunted, slaughtered, possibly for our role in the Great War. Why should we side with you in a war that may never come?"

"It is coming," Brandon replied, scraping a hand over his hair, frustration curdling his stomach. "It might already be here."

Silence passed between them, and then, "We are better with

our dragons. Without them, we do not fight." Khan paused, then pointed to the pendant. "Give that to your Ecix and see what she can do with it. Until then..."

Brandon held the medallion in his hand, then pocketed it. "Gather the rest of the riders. Find passage on ships to Cadira, or even get your own ships. And go to the mountains. The Ecix will protect you."

What Brandon didn't mention was that the Ecix likely wouldn't be there, that she was trapped in the capital. He didn't mention that the High Witch would try to turn them away. Brandon just needed to make it back, to give Eliza the news and the medallion.

Khan bowed his head and picked up the tea. After another sip, he said, "We shall see."

15

LEGENDS OF DEATH

Khan called a meeting for the rest of the clan to warn them of the coming Hunters. The fear Brandon had expected was muted, instead replaced with a heavy blanket of awareness. Aware they were still being hunted. Aware they would need to move again in order to remain safe. Brandon watched from the shadows as the elders and children were gathered and bundled in what they could carry, while the others strapped weapons—daggers of bones, steel swords, even bows and arrows dipped in what Khan told him was a paralysing agent they used to escape without killing—to their bodies, beneath the heavy layers of clothing.

Brandon helped as much as they would allow him to; the woman who had threatened him earlier stayed by his side as he bundled three of the children in their heavy coats, where they hid rations and water-skins for the elders. Brandon packed them bags that they could strap over their backs, light enough for them to run if needed to.

The children weren't nearly as afraid as they should be.

"You be careful," the old woman warned, pulling a small girl's hair out from beneath her hood. The little girl closed her eyes as the elder carefully braided it, as Brandon tightened the straps of her coat. "I heard from Khan you're staying behind."

Brandon looked up in surprise and found the old woman watching him. Her dark eyes narrowed, but not with anger. Curiosity, maybe. Even sadness.

He bowed his head and finished with the little girl. "I still have work to do here. I will hold the Hunters off for as long as I can."

"You should come with us. It would be better," she muttered.

Brandon looked up and met her stare. "But I still don't have what I came for."

Khan called his name. Brandon looked up and found the leader standing beneath a low-hanging branch; behind him was a short fence leading into what Brandon assumed to be a garden from the sprouting greens beyond Khan's figure. A soft smile played at the older man's lips as he motioned for Brandon to leave the elder and children.

The old woman looked as though she wanted to say more, but she tightened her lips into a thin line and resumed helping the children without looking up again.

Brandon rose with a sigh and followed Khan away from the group. He was not led back to the hut, but instead to a small garden. Khan knelt and began plucking ripe vegetables and fruits, roots and spices from the ground. "I never found out why you are here." He motioned to a woven basket, eyes trained on the garden before him.

Brandon hesitated, then knelt beside Khan. He watched the dragon rider pull vegetables from the ground, dark soil covering his calloused hands. Brandon considered a simple lie, but the truth slipped from his lips. "I came to Laziroth in search of an oracle," he replied slowly, reaching for the wicker basket, placing it in front of Khan.

The dragon rider leader smiled. "To my knowledge, there are no more."

Brandon bit the inside of his cheek, and contemplated whether telling him would be wise; on the one hand, Brandon trusted the leader, felt for him, but he didn't know the group well enough to entrust this mission with them. His only intent on finding them was to warn them about the Hunters and their location being exposed.

And yet, Brandon let the words fall from his lips. "Two hundred years ago, I found one. Here, in this valley. My...companion, a warlock, hid the oracle away. It should still be here, hidden in its den, but I just don't know where to look."

Khan looked up, eyes wide. "How do you expect to find it?"

"I've grown accustomed to his magic. I hope that if I search the ruins, I'll find the gateway," Brandon replied.

Khan stopped and rubbed his chin. "It would be an area of great magic, yes?"

Brandon nodded. "But you wouldn't be able to see anything physically. It should look unassuming."

"I may know where it is." Khan rose and wiped his hands. "I never realised we would be so close to an *oracle*."

Brandon stood. "Do you think you'll have time to tell me where it is?" he asked, a spark of hope entering his heart. But he was surprised that Khan hadn't been aware of the oracle. Had the legends truly died away over the years?

Khan met his stare with a smile. "I can show you."

~

They trekked down to the ruins, to the tree and its large roots. The symbols etched into the wood seemed so much greater than when Brandon had first seen them; he wondered if they represented safety for the riders, or something more. They were similar to the carvings he'd seen within the pixie circle.

Brandon didn't ask though, and instead followed Khan as they passed the original doorway.

After a moment of silence, Khan said, "If I had known an oracle still lived here, I would have sought it out much sooner." He paused by a tree; Brandon hadn't noticed it before, but there was another symbol carved into the wood. "When the Hunters realised there weren't many dragons left, some turned to the other magical beings that sought refuge in Laziroth. The oracles were either slaughtered or forced into servitude, merfolk were driven away from grottos so old they predated the dragons, the Little Folk disappeared. Soon magic in its entirety was wiped away."

They started again, and Brandon recognised the brush, the path they were walking. He frowned but followed, his mind racing. A deep sadness cut through him at how different the land was to his home. "Why didn't the riders escape? Go to the empire or Cadira?"

"We were afraid they would be worse." Khan shrugged. "It is easy now to say it would have been much simpler to run, and many did. I am sure there are many riders hiding on the other continents, on islands where their sea beasts sleep below the waves. But for those of us who remain, we remain because of our dragons."

Brandon pursed his lips; he wished Eliza were with him for all the history Khan was giving him. He knew she'd have a thousand questions for the leader, for their entire clan. But something Khan said reminded him of the tales he'd heard. "What do you mean by sleep? I remember being told stories about dragons sleeping within the mountains. I thought maybe all dragons slept."

"I wish it were that simple." Khan grunted as they began trekking up the mountain. "There was once a great clan who hid their dragons in the mountains. And with the aid of a powerful witch, they—along with their dragons—went to sleep, with a promise from this witch that she would wake them once there was peace. I do not know if this is fiction or truth. I assume the truth died during the hunt for necromancers."

Brandon hesitated before asking, "Was it the Ecix?"

"No." He shook his head. "All I know about her and her power is that after the Hunts, she wiped her hands clean of the dragons and the riders, and disappeared."

"One still sleeps in Cadira." Brandon stopped, the golden beast flashing across his memory, Eliza's fascination with it, the story Dorin had told them replaying in his ears. "At the palace. King Kamdon's dragon."

Khan flashed him a smile over his shoulder, like what Brandon had said was some sort of joke. "Perhaps she can tell you the truth, then." His voice turned soft as he said, "If I can move my clan safely, I would love to see her."

"I'm sure the king and Crown Prince would love to have you," Brandon replied, though he wasn't sure if he believed himself.

Khan considered it a moment, then shook his head. "Yes, I'm sure."

Brandon cracked a smile at Khan, who walked ahead. They hiked for several more minutes in silence; Brandon tried to bury his thoughts on dragons sleeping and hidden in pendants, and instead focus on what he needed to ask of the oracle, but as he stared at Khan's back, his mind wouldn't stop racing with what the rider had revealed.

They stopped near Brandon's camp, the outcropping of rocks slick with mildew. He furrowed his brow and looked around. "It's here?"

Khan frowned and nodded. "Yes, I'm sure. I believe it moves on occasion. I've felt its presence in multiple areas around the valley." Khan met his stare and shrugged. "I could be wrong, though. It has been a while since I've been surrounded by real magic, and not just parlour tricks from travellers escaping the villages of Hunters."

Brandon pursed his lips. He opened his senses for the magic; his guard dropped, and he let his own fears and thoughts fall away. The trick was not to seek it out; many made the mistake of begging for the magic to show itself. But magic lived, and like any creature, it was curious.

For a moment, nothing happened. And then...

The rock formation he had camped behind shifted, and a rock disappeared, revealing the entrance to a cave.

Khan released a breath. "My..."

Brandon palmed a dagger. "Thank you for showing me the way. I can go on from here."

Khan didn't move to leave, and instead offered his hand. "I wish you the best of luck."

Brandon clasped their hands before stepping forward. But the leader stopped him. "Why do you need to see the oracle if you are so sure of what this land's future holds?"

The commander sucked in a deep breath. "Because there has to be a way to stop this from happening. If war can be avoided..."

Khan bowed his head. "I understand." He took a step back. "We will wait, then, for you in the grove."

"No." Brandon shook his head. "Go ahead, and I will find you. Go to safety while you still have a chance."

Inside the cave, Brandon felt for a lantern; rust flaked in his hand, but the eternal flame still flickered within, just bright enough to illuminate his path.

From outside, Khan said, "I hope you find what you are looking for."

Brandon didn't look back; he closed his eyes, and sent a prayer to Azula as he entered the cave, and let the darkness close around him.

16

BEFORE

Brandon considered Amitel a moment as they followed the cart closely, keeping to the shadows of the trees. Enya, sitting alone at the head, guided the horses down the road. Completely alone, tears streaked through the soot on her face, hands trembling. She looked back at the crate and the oracle every so often, like she wasn't completely certain the creature was still locked away.

"We could take her out now," Brandon murmured, unsheathing the stolen sword. He and Amitel shared a look as they knelt within the brambles of a nearby bush. "She's an easy target." Brandon took a step towards the road.

Amitel pressed his lips into a thin line. "Wait."

Brandon paused at the edge of the road and frowned. "What?"

Uncertainty ignited in the warlocks' golden eyes as he stared at the young woman. Brandon hadn't had the chance to ask about their relationship, but he thought back to her words in the building, how she'd known how to trap him with the charm.

"Do you love her, Amitel?"

The warlock shook his head. "Once, I might have been able to. But she was always troubled, and I fear I might have played too much into her fantasies. Let me... let me try to reason with her."

Amitel spared him a pleading glance. "Please."

Brandon hesitated, warring voices in his mind telling him to put an end to the woman responsible for all the death and destruction, the other telling him to trust Amitel and his word.

The second voice won, and Brandon released a heavy breath, nodding. "Fine. Hurry."

Amitel bowed his head. "Wait here."

Clenching his jaw, Brandon watched Amitel dart down the road. The warlock was fast, inhuman, like a knight of the Brotherhood. Only his speed and strength came from somewhere else. A spell, magic of some kind. Or perhaps the warlock was more than met the eye.

After a moment, Brandon followed, remaining in the shadows. Ahead, the cart came to a halt. The horses reacted to Amitel's imposing figure, but they stilled mid-air with shimmering, golden magic.

Brandon stopped within hearing distance, hand straying to the sword on his hip. Enya scrambled from her seat into the back of the cart, pressing herself into the wood of the crate. "What are you doing, Amitel?" she asked, voice quivering.

Amitel raised his hands in surrender. "Please, Enya, let us talk about this. Let me take you somewhere safe, away from all of this."

She shook her head. "No, I have to show her. I have to *prove she was wrong!*" Enya rubbed a hand over her face and covered her eyes; Amitel's gaze flickered to where Brandon stood in the shadows and gave a soft shake of his head in warning.

But Brandon tightened his grip around his sword and took a step. Enya's head shot up, and she searched the road, frantic eyes taking in everything...but him. Brandon frowned as she cowered into the crate more.

"If I do not return with the oracle, I am as good as dead," she whispered. "I have been abandoned by my men, by my family." Her eyes turned glassy as they returned to Amitel. "By *you.* If I can get this monster back to the Courts, then I can get it all back."

Amitel shook his head. "That's not how this works, Enya." He took a tentative step forward, raising his hands. "You know that."

She screamed in frustration and threw a jagged steel dagger at Amitel. He ducked out of its path, and it clattered to the ground.

Brandon rushed from the trees, sword outstretched as Enya curled in on herself, tears of blood slipping down her sooty cheeks.

The warlock threw up his hand and stopped Brandon from taking another step. Enya made no move to attack Amitel again, but Brandon didn't want to risk it. Instead, he rounded the cart, inching closer to her shuddering frame.

"I have to go back," she whispered, rubbing the palms of her hands into her eyes. "I have to go back. I have to go back. *I have to go back.*"

Brandon sent Amitel a look, raising a brow. But the warlock's concerned gaze was on the girl.

Enya dropped her hands and met Amitel's stare. She rose on shaky knees, hands tightened into fists. "You're right, Amitel." She took a step, like she planned to jump from the cart. "This isn't how it works."

Brandon didn't see the second dagger at first; the blade entered her left hand, sliding free from beneath her sleeve, and flipped from her fingers in the direction of the warlock. Brandon shouted, but the dagger grazed Amitel's shoulder as he ducked out of his path. Enya pulled a third free.

Before Brandon could leap onto the cart, the girl froze, her eyes going wide. The dagger fell from rigid fingers and clattered to the floor of the cart. Her body tensed, a choking sound leaving her lips. Amitel lifted a hand and held it out to her. "I'm sorry," he murmured. A spell, whispered in a tongue none but witches and warlocks knew, spilled from his lips. Golden magic wove over his skin towards his outstretched hands, and ignited in his burning eyes.

Enya shuddered and collapsed, her hands clutching her abdomen tightly. A scream tore from her throat as a soft golden light shimmered across her skin. It grew brighter, consuming her clothing, the copper of her hair, until her entire figure was gold. Warmth radiated from her trembling frame.

Brandon shielded his eyes until it dimmed, and the girl who had once been encapsulated in the light was gone.

He dropped his hands and turned to Amitel, who leaned heavily against the side of the cart, breathing jagged, blood tingeing his upper lip. "Are you alright?" Brandon asked.

Amitel's eyes dropped closed as he nodded. "I'll be fine." He swallowed heavily and lifted his head. Gone was the gold that swam in his irises, leaving only crimson in its place. "Let's take this creature back to its temple and pray to the Gods no one else finds it."

~

"Where did she go?" Brandon asked as the barge carried them and the oracle across the lake. He stared down at his blackened hands as the crate behind him rattled with the oracle's movements.

Amitel joined him at the edge of the barge. "Somewhere safe." He leaned into the railing and bowed his head. "Somewhere she won't hurt anyone else."

Brandon clamped his mouth shut and said nothing. Amitel's words from earlier replayed in his mind, of his guilt and anger towards not only Enya and the oracle, but at himself. Perhaps if he hadn't given into the anger, into the darkness of his heart, he wouldn't have been part of the destruction of Varun, wouldn't have given into Enya's delusions of war.

When he turned towards the village, only the cathedral was left standing, the stone darkened by soot. The town that had once been raised by stilts over the lake now crumbled, reclaimed by the waters that had once sustained it. The fires had stopped burning, like Enya's disappearance had killed the flames, but the destruction remained, illuminated by the rising sun.

The people of Varun gathered at the shore and helped them dock the barge. Their tired faces were thankful, but Brandon knew he'd done nothing to help them. The kings of Laziroth would not send their soldiers to help the small village rebuild.

Brandon swallowed hard as he and Amitel climbed atop the cart and prepared for the days ahead. The trek to the valley would be hard with the added weight of the cart and oracle, but the chains that had once bound the creature were broken, trapped within the temple, and only the crate protected them from its ancient magic.

A villager stepped in the path of the horses, the same man that had helped ferry survivors from the fire to the shore. "Where do you go now?" he asked, arms crossed. Those who survived gathered around him.

Brandon and Amitel shared a look. "We will return what they stole back to its rightful place," Amitel replied. "Then I will return to help you rebuild."

The villagers whispered amongst themselves, moving away from the cart. The man lifted his chin. "We have lost everything to those mercenaries, to that girl."

"I know." Amitel bowed his head, releasing a breath. "And I know I cannot replace everything she stole, but I can give you my magic, my time, to rebuild what she destroyed."

"Magic got us here," the man sneered. "Magic will not fix this."

Amitel met his stare. "I am aware of that, and I would not expect it to. I will help in any way you need. But first, we must return this."

He didn't wait for a response, and rolled the reins. The cart lurched forward, and those still in the path of the horses moved out of their way with wide, fearful eyes.

Brandon waited until they were out of earshot of the villagers before speaking. "You surprise me, warlock," he said, watching Amitel from the corner of his eye. "Do you have the energy to do what you promised?"

Amitel rolled his shoulders back. "The fire is gone, and Enya's charm is wearing off. Once I've had a few days' rest, I'll be back to my normal enchanting self."

17

THE ORACLE

The darkness was eerily familiar as Brandon approached the destroyed portions of the once majestic temple. He climbed over pillars coated in thick layers of moss, avoiding the remains of statues claimed by pools of water. The heavy dust he remembered was gone; somewhere, deep within, water dripped, and the air smelt damp, different.

Was it Amitel's magic that changed the temple, or time? Brandon paused and knelt to pick up an old, broken chain. It had been the only thing truly powerful enough to trap the oracle in the old temple, the one thing that should have stopped anyone from releasing the creature back into the world. There were horrible stories about oracles using their power to destroy kingdoms and empires before they were ever born, how their ability to see into the future caused more destruction than any war. Once, long ago, a Queen had decided, with the help of a God, to lock the oracles away in temples so that only the worthy could meet with them. Brandon wasn't sure if that part of the history was true, or if the oracles themselves had gone into hiding, knowing their fate.

The last time he'd seen the chains, they'd been around the oracle's neck.

A flash of silver caught Brandon's eye; it wasn't a chain, but rather an old dagger. The blade fell apart like sand in his hands, but he recognised the make. It was a weapon of the Brotherhood—it should never fault, and yet that one had.

He rose. Something had certainly changed in the temple.

A path cut through the debris and he followed it, finding himself walking a narrow bridge through a river. The further he walked, the deeper it became, the depths darker, less certain. There had never been water so far in. Around him there should have been statues and crypts, but they were gone, lost to the depths of the dark river on either side of him.

He held up the lantern; the light flickered every so often, throwing strange shadows over the walls. At some point, the oracle—before his first trip into the temple with Amitel—had used the bone of someone unworthy to carve the future into the walls.

The scenes were gruesome; Brandon paused at the bent figure of Celia, who cradled her dead sister in her arms while the Faery Knight and raven watched with bowed heads. Another scene, one he hadn't paid much attention to before, now made sense: an open window with billowing curtains, a cradle empty of an infant, a woman lying dead reaching for the assassin sent to steal her son.

A shiver worked its way down his spine as he continued on the path.

If he had paid more attention to what the oracle had said and done, maybe things would have been different.

Brandon continued on the path, keeping his eyes peeled for anything else that might prove useful. But the other scenes were destroyed. Ones he remembered being full were now cracked and crumbling, while others scratched and torn apart by someone's hand. He paused at the remains of an old image; two women riding into battle, one with a blazing sword, the other dripping darkness. It had been scratched away, but he remembered the brilliance it once was.

The sound of rattling chains made him stop.

"Brandon..." it called, making him freeze. "*I know you're there. I sense your future. Would you like to see it?*"

He clenched his jaw. The fire flickered out for a moment, and when it reignited, he was no longer on the path.

Brandon found himself standing at the end of the tunnel, in a crumbling cavern with only the light of his torch to illuminate his surroundings. He sidestepped the head of a statue as he searched for the oracle, but the darkness was thick as the edges of the flickering fire.

Chains rattled behind him, and he spun. Hidden in a small alcove, a hunched figure with wide, unblinking silver eyes watched him. Sharp teeth flashed a wicked smile, and he took a step back as the child lunged.

It wore the face of a little girl with mousy brown curls, but talons replaced her fingers. Mildew coated its skin, and in some places, moss grew. Vines with golden thorns wove along thin, gangly arms and legs, over the rags of a dress yellowed with age. Chains like the ones he'd found near the entrance were clasped around the child's ankles and neck, keeping it close to the wall.

The oracle struggled against its chains. *"What is it you seek this time, immortal soldier?"*

Brandon lifted his chin and unsheathed his sword. The sight of the ancient creature took him back to after the resurgence, of the darkness in his heart and the terrible lengths he would have gone to in order to forget. "The truth," he said, blood thundering in his ears.

The girl cocked her head. *"About the girl you love or her enemy?"*

His breath caught in his throat, but he pushed his fear for Eliza—for Isolde—aside. "Both."

"And?" A wicked smile played at her blackened lips.

"And how can I find the dagger?"

The image of the child shimmered in front of him; he knew now that it only revealed itself in its most vulnerable form, so those who sought to hurt it would think twice. A defence mechanism that didn't fool him, and wouldn't again.

He'd seen it for the grotesque creature it was. And he and Amitel had trapped it once before.

"Well?" he asked, stepping forward, bringing the tip of his blade to the child's throat. "Show me the future."

Silver turned black as its eyes met his. *"Very well."*

The cavern shook; somewhere behind him, glass shattered as the walls threatened to cave in. Brandon stumbled back as darkness edged at his vision.

"*You seek Azula's Dagger,*" it said. The oracle closed its eyes; the temple fell completely silent around them, stilling. "*I cannot see it. Not its past, present, or future.*"

Brandon paced the length of the oracle's resting place; it was a small room within the cavern at the end of the path, the walls a destructive scene that had been erased and redrawn over and over again. The bones of some poor creature were stacked in the corner, as well as weapons that turned to dust when he kicked them.

He came to a stop and turned to face the child. "What do you mean?"

She shrugged her small shoulders, the movement so strange he had to blink and remember the being in front of him wasn't really a child, but a creature as old as the land he stood on. "*It is beyond my capabilities.*"

He frowned, hand tightening on the hilt of his sword. "Try harder."

The oracle's black eyes followed him as he began pacing again; he felt its gaze burning into the side of his head, but he didn't stop. An archway at least three times his height looked ready to fall and trap the oracle in its small room, but magic—or something else—held it together.

"*It may have been and it may never have been. History lies and stories reveal truths,*" the oracle said, the words barely a whisper, but the room carried its voice well enough that Brandon never had to stop his pacing.

"What does that mean?" he asked, touching a hand to his forehead.

"*It may be a weapon of the gods or a figment of mortal imagination. There is no truth or lie to its existence.*"

"It has to be real." He stopped again and turned to the girl. "The Ecix almost had it."

The child shrugged again. "*I do not see it. Not in her future or yours.*"

Brandon bit the inside of his cheek as he shook his head. *No,* he thought, resuming his pacing. *This isn't why I am here. I came for answers, not this.*

He had left Eliza's side so he could find a way to stop the Dark Master without risking Eliza's life. He'd left believing it was the only way to aid her in her search.

But had he been wrong?

Had he failed?

"What *do* you see for her?" he asked finally.

"*A terrible war.*" The oracle paused, and something changed on its face as it closed its eyes. "*Death. So much death.*" The oracle visibly shuddered, like what it saw frightened even them. "*An adversary unlike any she's encountered.*" The oracle reopened its eyes. "*What I saw for her has come to pass. Now, there are shadows and light. So much light. But it could either be her saviour—or her ruin.*"

Something dropped into the pit of his stomach. Brandon pressed his back into the edge of the archway and dropped to the ground, letting his head fall back against the damp stone.

"Was it you who warned me last night?" he asked softly, knowing she would hear him.

"*The past Ecix entered your dreams,*" the oracle replied, shrugging. "*I merely used it to pass on a warning.*"

He didn't say anything as his stomach churned. Brandon closed his eyes. For a moment, he let the silence wash over him; everything he'd learnt and hadn't. The purpose of his mission had been to find an alternative, and yet the oracle could see nothing about the dagger.

"Is there a way to stop the Dark Master?" he asked. "To kill him without the dagger?"

When he opened his eyes, he found the oracle watching him. "*No,*" it replied. "*I see no way to destroy him without the Ecix.*"

His heart stammered in his chest as he asked, "What will she need to do?"

But the oracle shook her head. "*I cannot see it.*"

He bit his lip. "You said he knows the truth. Did you mean the Dark Master?"

The oracle's eyes flickered back to silver and met his. "*Yes.*"

"What truth does he know?"

"*That is murky. I am unable to see him clearly.*" The oracle pressed its lips into a line.

Brandon blew out a hot breath. "Is there anything else I should know? About my friends?"

"Their futures are murky. There is something standing in their way..." the oracle trailed off. *"I do not see anything clearly. Only war. Only destruction. It will reclaim this land, and it will either be its obliteration—or its liberator."*

Brandon rose sharply and strode over to where the oracle sat. "What do you mean?"

The creature looked up and met his stare; something like fear glinted in its black eyes. *"There is no future beyond the war."*

Brandon tightened his hand into a fist. "Did Amitel tell the truth? Did you tell him to betray Eliza?"

The creature smiled. *"He did as fate commanded—as the God's commanded."* Head cocked, it scurried closer and nipped at him with sharpened teeth. *"There will be a girl with great power. An Ecix. And she will be hunted and broken before she can rise. But she will be betrayed. By* him." A broken laugh poured from its lips as Brandon shoved it back with the tip of his sword.

"Betrayed she was, as betrayal will strike again." The oracle glared up at Brandon with dark eyes. *"Will you be the hero she needs, Brandon Thorne?"*

Jaw clenched, Brandon paused, a breath shuddering from his lips. He couldn't breathe; he stepped away from the oracle, then walked back towards the path, picking up the discarded lantern. His fist tightening around the hilt of his sword.

"Do you not wish to know your fate?" the oracle called before he could take one step onto the path.

He paused, and said over his shoulder, "I'm not sure."

Amitel's warnings of fate and oracles played in the back of his mind, but the words from Eliza's letter forced him to turn around and stop in front of the oracle once more.

"It will help your friends. But it will destroy you."

Brandon closed his eyes, levelling his breathing. Every inch of him told him not to allow the creature into his head, that he should not let his future drown him.

And yet, he opened his eyes. If he could be a master of his own fate, shouldn't he take that chance?

18

THE DRAGON

The oracle's words followed Brandon as he left the ruins. He walked until he saw the light of day, dropped the lantern inside the cave, and didn't look back.

Dusk coated the sky, visible through the canopy of leaves, painting it lilac and gold. How much time had passed, he wondered, since he'd been in the valley? From memory, he recalled that time worked differently in the den. It could have been days or minutes for all he knew. Years, if fate wanted to play cruel tricks on him.

He wondered how far the riders had gotten, if they had made it out of the valley safely. He hoped they had.

Brandon stopped at the foot of the old entrance and fell to his knees. He dropped his sword into the grass at his feet and stared at the thick blood still coating the blade's edge.

The oracle had lifted its head in greeting, as if knowing its life would end by his sword.

Brandon's head thrummed with the knowledge of his future. It felt worse, somehow, knowing what was to come, knowing his own purpose in the war. Perhaps giving him insight into the darkness of his own destiny was his punishment.

He wasn't sure if knowing was better than not knowing.

Brandon squeezed his eyes shut and lowered his head as he sucked in cooling breaths. His thoughts raced with everything the oracle had said, but the creature had been firm with its words: his future would come to pass no matter what he tried to change, and his future would benefit the war—and Eliza.

It didn't stop him from wishing things would be different.

There is much you will sacrifice for the Ecix, the oracle had said, *and this will be the greatest of all.*

Slowly, he rose and stared down at the sword. He'd done what was necessary, and yet his stomach churned. But at least he knew the oracle would not fall into the hands of the Dark Master. As he bent to retrieve the sword, he wondered what his friends would say about his actions.

Brandon shook his head and wiped the blade clean of blood. He would not tell them. They didn't need to know of the lengths he'd gone to in order to protect them.

He stumbled away from the tree in the direction of the grove; he wanted some time to be alone, but being out in the open was a risk he knew he shouldn't take.

The grove would be empty, the silence inviting. It would be hidden enough to give him some time to himself before he met with the riders; at least he'd be able to start a fire, have shelter for the night. If he was lucky, there'd still be some food he could cook up for supper.

A shout made him pause.

Brandon hadn't sensed anyone else in the valley, but now, as he stilled himself, he felt the presence of many. Conflicting magic crawled over his skin and the hairs on his arms rose.

He wasn't alone.

And the riders hadn't left.

Brandon stalked through the forest, keeping to the thick trunks of trees, listening for more. A small opening in the heavy brush revealed too many people; riders and Hunters alike, gathered together, ready for an execution.

The commander paused and pressed into the tree; the children were gathered and being held by three Hunters, while the elders and fighters were on their knees, their hands behind their backs. Brandon spied Khan, the old woman at his side. They both shared looks of defiance.

The hunter Brandon had encountered in Varun appeared, grinning and pleased with himself. He wore heavy armour around his chest and torso, leaving his forearms bare. The tattoos and proof of his kills stood stark against his tanned flesh.

Brandon's shoulders tensed as the hunter stopped in front of Khan. "Your deaths will be swift," he said, like that would benefit his captives, "and your deaths will be for the empire!"

The empire... The Hunters believed themselves far greater than what they actually were. Brandon couldn't help but roll his eyes as the smug bastard used the tip of a dragon bone blade to lift Khan's chin.

Brandon slid his sword free from its sheath and palmed a dagger. There were two Hunters closest to him; he could take both down in one swift motion. He knew Khan would have many more weapons on him, hidden beneath the layers of his clothing, and Brandon hoped the other riders did, too.

But he hesitated, fear for the children stopping him before he could move. The Hunters, he hoped, would be too focused on him and the adults that they would release the children. He hoped they would run.

Brandon rolled his shoulders back. He let thoughts of the oracle fall into a chest, and he tucked it away with the others. It was not important, not at that moment.

The lives in front of him were.

With his mind set, Brandon threw the first dagger. Two Hunters fell, and another rushed Brandon before anyone could process his arrival. Years of training and honing his strength and speed made the fight all the easier for him; he ducked blows and dealt many of his own before there was any retaliation from the Hunters.

Riders leapt to their feet as their captors rushed Brandon. He lifted his sword as the adults brandished their own weapons, while elders ran to gather the children and hide.

Brandon sliced through the mock armour the Hunters wore, blood pounding so loud in his ears it became a familiar song of battle. He wondered if he had been the one to lead them to the riders. Had they followed him from the inn, traced his steps to the valley? Did they watch him find the entrance to the grove? When he and Khan left for the oracle? Had they waited until he was occupied to go after the riders?

He didn't let the questions stop him; Brandon swept beneath the arm of a hunter and sliced through the man's abdomen, and didn't look back to see if he succumbed to his wound.

From the corner of his eye, he spied a hunter leaving the fight; Brandon palmed a dagger, but before he could throw it, a bone knife pierced the hunter's back. He fell like a log, and did not move again.

Brandon spun to face Khan; blood ran from a cut above his eye and from his nose. Shadows rolled over the clearing, and the sky darkened with the threat of a storm. The once clear day turned grey, dangerous. In the distance, over the song of swords, thunder rumbled, lightning streaking across the clouds.

The gods had been angered, but did they cry for the Hunters, or seek vengeance for the dragons?

"Are you alright?" Brandon asked the Dragon Rider. Guilt curdled in Brandon's stomach as Khan bent to retrieve a fallen bone sword. He winced, straightening, hand hovering over his side.

Khan fell into step beside Brandon. "I thought I wouldn't see you again," the rider said, giving Brandon a half smile.

"I thought I'd see you up the mountain," Brandon replied, grunting as a hunter slammed into him. His sword slipped from his hand, but he used the momentum to pull a dagger from his belt and slam it upwards into the Hunter's ribcage. The man dropped, and Brandon fell back into rhythm with Khan.

"I will be honest," the rider said, his gaze flickering over the corpses filling the clearing. "I thought you brought them here. Used us to make us to leave."

Brandon paused, sparing him a glance, his breath shuddering from his lips. "I'm sorry."

"Why?" Khan stopped as well, brow furrowing. "I assume I wasn't correct. You returned and are helping us now."

"I still could have led them here, even unwillingly. Perhaps you would have been safer in the grove, at least until I returned."

"It wouldn't have protected us forever."

Brandon said nothing to that. Although Khan was right, it

didn't stop the guilt. Maybe Brandon should have asked the oracle for the fate of the riders, for Khan's sake.

He should have done many things differently, he knew now.

Brandon pulled Khan out of the way of another hunter, dragging the leader behind him so he would take the brunt of the impact. Brandon released a breath as a rib cracked in his chest, but he swung out, dagger still in hand, and lodged it into the gut of the hunter. This time, Brandon did not pull it from the body.

Over the field of bodies, Brandon spied the leader of the Hunters; rage crossed the man's face as their gazes met over the fight. Bloodlust filled his dark eyes, one Brandon recognised. It was a bloodlust that he'd shoved deep down, swore never to let resurface. But the hunter wore it like a badge, held it like a weapon.

The hunter stalked forward. Brandon started for the man, unsheathing two new daggers as he did. The hunter only grinned and freed his own. The mist of battle curled over Brandon's mind as they met in the middle of the field, their blades clashing as the sky opened. Rain fell in a heavy sheet, but Brandon had fought under worse conditions. The forest floor turned to mud, but he dug his boots in, tightening his grip on the sword.

The hunter rushed Brandon with his sword raised, a yell passing his lips. Sword raised, Brandon met the blow and moved back before the hunter could strike again. They circled one another as thunder drowned out the cries on either side. But blood pounded in Brandon' ears as he stared the hunter down.

Warmth filled Brandon's veins, anticipation sweeping through him. The noise of battle fell away, leaving Brandon alone with the hunter.

Every clash of their blades made his bones rattle, but he fell into a familiar rhythm, a dance his muscles knew without instruction.

Brandon swiped, aiming for the Hunter's gut, but the man danced back and returned with another blow. The blade sung by Brandon's ear as he arched back out of reach, but he raised his blade to meet the hunter's next strike. Brandon dropped his dagger, leaving it for the slick mud, and instead grasped the pommel with both hands.

Their swords met again; Brandon used the momentum to kick

the hunter away and watched the man stumble into the mud, his dagger falling. The anger that swept his features only grew darker, ravenous. The hunter aimed his sword up and leapt to his feet, almost skewering Brandon with the blade, but the commander spun out of reach.

"Are you tiring yet, soldier?" the hunter growled, dragging his hand over his eyes, wiping away sweat and rain.

Brandon rolled his shoulders. "I'm a knight of the Brotherhood. We do not tire."

The fury in his opponent's eyes almost made Brandon stop, but it was the fear that caught him off guard. He sidestepped another blow as he took the hunter in; the tall, muscular frame and years of training made him a worthy rival, but the weight of his blows were weakening, and with each strike, he grew frantic. Worried.

The hunter bared his teeth, and with a grunt, he threw his full weight into the next strike. It caught Brandon off guard, and he fell, rolling in time to miss the blow that would have pierced his heart. He jumped to his feet to avoid another slice from the Hunter's blade. Sweat burned the back of his neck despite the frigid rain blurring his vision and chilling his skin.

Khan ducked in front of Brandon, cutting him off from the hunter. "This one is mine," Khan said, their eyes meeting briefly.

Under his breath, Brandon swore, but he made no argument. The hunter was Kahn's kill, and Brandon understood that.

Another hunter appeared at Brandon's right, the steel of his blade coated red. The man grinned, revealing sharpened teeth. Tattoos, faded from years in the sun, lined his skull like a crown. A list of kills.

Brandon flipped his blade as the hunter growled.

"This is for my family," Khan shouted behind him, blades striking, "for my clan."

The sound of metal sliding through flesh made Brandon turn; he expected to find the hunter on the other end of a sword, but instead, he came face to face with the bloodied edge of a blade, which cut through Khan and slid free a moment later.

The hunter grinned. "And that was for *me*."

Fury burned in Brandon's veins as he caught Khan's falling body. Cries rose up from the remaining riders, several of who dropped their weapons and fell to their knees. Others fought with a vengeance unlike anything Brandon had ever witnessed, cutting through Hunters in their attempts to get to the one responsible for their leader's death.

Brandon lowered Khan to the ground. His dark eyes found Brandon's, tears brimming the corners, spilling onto his muddy cheeks. His lips trembled as he tried to form words.

"I have failed," he whispered, eyes flickering up to the sky. "I did not save them."

"You did," Brandon replied, trying to ignore the boiling of his blood. "You protected them."

Khan met his stare, blood bubbling from his lips. "I doomed them."

The light dimmed in his dark eyes, and his head lolled to the side. Brandon lifted his bloody hand and closed Khan's eyes. He did not know what else to do as he lowered the man to the ground. Clenching his jaw, Brandon looked up at the hunter responsible.

The other riders fought their way to him, but Brandon was closer. He found his sword nearby and dove, rolling as he pulled it from the ground. The hunter swung down with his blade—a blade still dripping with Khan's blood. The weapons sang as they connected, but Brandon pushed back, throwing the hunter off guard.

There was a reserve of strength deep within him. Brandon rarely accessed it, but he pulled from it as he swung, each strike hitting the blade of the hunter. Each time, his opponent grew weaker and weaker. Brandon called on the magic in his blood to give him the strength to end the hunter in front of him.

Brandon sheathed his sword, freed a dagger, and used his fist for the final blow, knuckles connecting with the Hunter's jaw.

He shoved the hunter into a tree, pressing a dagger to the man's throat. "I won't kill you now," Brandon hissed, letting the edge dig into his throat. "Because your death shouldn't be on my hands."

"A coward, are you, knight?" The hunter lifted a brow, but his lips trembled.

"No." Brandon pressed the knife deeper into his throat. "Because there is a line of people who wish to see you bleed out, so

I won't be the one to take it from them." Brandon pushed away from the hunter, dropping the dagger in favour of his sword. He raised it to the man's throat, which bobbed. "No, I won't kill you. They won't either. Not today. Your death will come, and when it does, you won't know. You will spend the rest of your useless, miserable life looking over your shoulder, waiting for that knife in your back."

The Hunter's eyes darkened as Brandon lowered his blade. "You will return to the empire. And you won't come after me, or the riders again. You'll retire." He sheathed his blade and stepped back. "If you try to hurt anyone here—myself included—you will wish I had granted you death. Because if the wrong person learns of your wrong doings here today, death will not be the release you believe it is."

Hatred burned in the dark eyes of the hunter. Around them, the riders tied up the Hunters who had assaulted and held them captive, none saying a word as the Hunters fell into line. But their quiet cries followed Brandon as he lifted Khan into his arms and carried him away from the battlefield.

19

THE PIRATES RESCUE

Brandon touched the old woman's shoulder. "I'm sorry."

She blinked up at him, but it seemed as though she couldn't see him. Tears brimmed her dark, tired eyes. "I know."

Three riders carried Khan towards a small pyre built within the ruins of the old temple. The children had cleared away the moss to reveal the old, cracked stone, and with the help of the elders, they gathered dry wood and sticks to create a funeral pyre.

There were six dead, including Khan. Nameless riders. Brandon would ask their names later once they left the valley.

The dead Hunters were left for their leader to deal with once he managed to untie himself. Those not dead were chained to trees. Part of him wished they would not find a way to free themselves, that they would rot in the same forest they had believed themselves the predators of.

No, Brandon thought, shaking his head. The thought stuck with him, though.

If it weren't for the small clan, he might've considered returning to finish the job. Put an end to them before they could hurt anyone else.

Instead, Brandon let the elder lean against him as the women of the clan began a low chant. Men, injured and bloody, straightened as another elder stopped at each of them to light a torch.

"The fire will return them to the dragons," the old woman said, her voice a whisper as she watched the men carry the torches to the pyre. It reminded Brandon of a Keeper's funeral, how the burning of the physical body allowed for the person's magic to return to the land. But he hadn't considered what fire would mean for the dragon riders.

The women shouted as lightning cracked against the sky. The movement of the electricity almost looked like a dragon.

Around Brandon, the dragon riders hummed, heads lowered as the men dropped the burning torches onto the pyre. Within the blink of an eye, almost like a dragon had released a breath, fire consumed the pyre, engulfing the bodies and carrying them into the land of death.

Brandon closed his eyes and mouthed a prayer of the Brotherhood. He asked for forgiveness from Azula and her guidance as they entered her realm.

As the chants came to an end, Brandon opened his eyes. The fire died, dwindling to embers. The old man said something in a low voice as the women gathered the ashes and swept them into yellowed boxes.

"What do we do now?" the old woman asked, staring up at Brandon. "We have nowhere to go. Khan had the next location planned."

"Do you trust me?" Brandon asked. "Enough to find you somewhere safe?"

The elder looked between him and the rest of the clan; the thoughts played along her features, a whirlwind of questions and scenarios that she would have to live with. Could she trust him? Or could she find them the shelter and safety they needed?

Injured warriors tended to their wounds, while exhausted elders cared for tearful children. They were too young to understand the severity of what was happening to them, and yet Brandon knew they little ones understood, to some degree, the destruction of the hunters.

Brandon wanted to help, but he would leave them if they asked.

Finally, the woman sighed, dropping her shoulders. "Where will you take us?"

"To a ship," he replied, "and then to safety."

~

They made it to a port before sunset as ships came into dock and fishing vessels packed up for the night. A soft lull of music drifted down the tired streets from a tavern nestled on the shoreline, while a bonfire ignited on a small patch of beach near the docks. Brandon remained ahead of the clan to make sure no Hunters crossed their paths, but it seemed the large port city was free of them.

He motioned for the clan to follow him to the water's edge; he fished through his pack for the stone Captain Piper had given him. As the sun dipped below the horizon, he threw it into the ocean and watched it sink into the dark blue depths.

"What are you doing?" the old woman asked, stepping up beside him.

Brandon looked up from the water and stared out at the horizon. "Calling on a friend." He turned to the woman, who pressed her lips into a thin line. "A pirate. She'll take you and the clan somewhere safe."

The old woman's brows drew together. "And you? Where will you go?"

"Home." As he said, he knew exactly what he needed to do. "There is much to be done."

"Khan warned me of what you told him," she said. "I know about this war, what you asked of him." She looked behind her at the rest of the clan, who drew close to one another. "I do not know if it is possible, not in our shape."

"I understand."

She sighed. "There are others. Khan's daughter. She was supposed to be with us. But she and several others left to be heroes." Brandon tensed as the old woman continued, "I do not know where she is, if she is even alive. If they will find us."

"Do you have a way of contacting her? Is there something I can do?" he asked.

The woman shook her head. "No. If they are out there, they will find us. Clan will always find clan." A smile played on her thin lips.

He said nothing more as they waited.

The dreaded *Voyager* appeared under the cover of night when a soft mist curled over the still ocean. Either they had been close, or magic had something to do with their quick appearance. If the stories were true, pirates had learnt of charms to enchant their sails so they could take the oceans like a storm. Someone like the *Voyager's* captain was surely capable of doing the same.

The ship docked, with Piper taking the lead disembarking, with Osiris and the young boy Brandon saved at her side.

He met them on the dock, leaving the riders behind. "Thank you for coming."

Her eyes were curious as she looked between him and the group, dwindled down to fourteen. "My offer was to help *you*, not misfits you happen to pick up on your travels." She drew her brows in a frown. "What is going on?"

"I need your help to get them to safety." Before she could open her mouth, he continued, "They're being hunted. And I think you know why."

A moment ticked by as she looked between him and the clan. Her eyes widened as the realisation clicked. "Dragon Riders?" She rubbed a hand over her face. "You're an idiot, Brandon Thorne," Piper said, shaking her head. "You know why I was even there on Crane's ship?"

Something twisted in his gut, but she held up a hand. "I was paid to destroy his ship in retribution for his assault on some Hunters. *That's* why I was there."

"But you don't agree with them, do you?" Brandon asked. "You don't agree with the Hunters?"

She was silent a moment, lips pursed, but eventually, she shook her head. "No. It was easy coin, and I loathed Crane, anyway. He's done worse to these people."

Brandon tensed. "Will you take them to safety?"

Her bright eyes danced between him and the group, then sighed. "Yes." She motioned for Osiris and said, "Get them on board. Clean out the captain's quarters and let them stay in there. Set a course for the southern peninsular."

Something like relief crossed his features, and he nodded.

"Aye, captain."

"And you?" Piper asked as Osiris left for the ship, turning back to the commander. "Will you go with them?"

Brandon shook his head. "My fate lies across the ocean in Cadira."

"I've heard tales from Cadira," she warned, stepping away. "Terrible ones. You should prepare yourself."

Jaw clenched, Brandon gave her a nod. "I don't expect things to be the same as when I left," he replied, "but I hope for a chance to make amends with those I left behind."

The captain glanced over at him with a raised brow. "Good luck," she replied. "But my offer stands. It may be easier for these people if you travel with them."

"I've been gone long enough." Brandon set his gaze out over the ocean. "I think it's time I finally face my destiny."

~

With the riders on board the *Voyager*, Brandon remained to seek out a ship to return him to Port Hein. It took him several hours to coax out a vessel, but eventually he found a Cadiran ship set to leave before sun up, the captain more than happy to help one of King Bastian's own soldiers.

On board, Brandon was left to his thoughts, which were a flurry of questions and what ifs.

The oracle's warnings played on a loop in the back of his mind as he leaned against the mainmast, night blanketing the land. Another day of sailing stood between him and Cadira. It would come to pass—his future, and he knew it would have to if they wanted to win the war.

A war that crept closer every day.

Something certainly had happened, like Captain Piper had warned; the crew of the *Mathilde* were quiet, solemn, their sadness like a stench of death. But Brandon couldn't get an answer out of anyone, and it ate at him with each passing day.

A letter from Celia arrived two days into his journey, though not even she revealed much in her words. He'd asked for her to meet him in Port Hein, and all she could reply with was: *I will be there.*

His questions strayed from his future, to the present; had Eliza married Alicsar? He expected to feel the excitement of the crew if it had happened. Which made him wonder if something else had happened in the days since he'd last spoken to Eliza.

Could so much change so quickly?

He remembered her letter and thought, *yes*. She would have married Alicsar. She was likely on their wedding tour, visiting the different towns and villages that made up Cadira. Part of her would be hating it, but another would be enjoying the escape from the palace.

Brandon crossed his arms over his chest as he took in the constellations of Cadira and the twin moons that guided them. There were two others on deck, but they didn't bother him, and he made no effort to speak to them.

The questions did not take over; Brandon did not let them.

Instead, he let the gentle rock of the ship lull him into the present, leaving thoughts of the past behind.

20

BEFORE

Brandon heaved a breath as they made it into the valley. Sweat beaded his brow, lining the back of his neck, and he wiped his mouth as they approached the site of the temple.

The entrance shimmered, opening to reveal a cavern, illuminated only by the light of a torch within the cave's mouth. The eternal flame flickered as they entered, the crate carrying the oracle floating behind them.

Brandon stopped just inside to take the torch, warmed by the flame, but not burnt from centuries spent alight. "Will we be able to chain it up?" he asked, spying a length of dull chain left by the mercenaries.

Ahead, Amitel stopped by a statue, his frame outlined by the dim light of the torch. "My magic should suffice," he replied. "I can rework the original spell to rebind it to the temple."

Brandon didn't respond, and followed the warlock further into the cavern. Statues of old heroes and Gods of Laziroth surrounded a raised platform made of limestone. Sand dusted a crypt and the face of the stone queen. Columns that had once been standing now lie in the dirt.

The torch guided them down a path of crypts and strange

carvings in the stone walls. Brandon lowered his gaze from them, Isolde's death a permanent reminder etched into the cavern.

Neither spoke until the torch flickered off, leaving them in darkness for only a moment. Shadows dispersed as the light brightened, revealing a small alcove where the oracle had once been chained, and the binds that had trapped Amitel and Brandon within.

He looked away and found a sconce, leaving the torch within. Ignoring the scattered bones and rusted weapons, Brandon approached the crate, which gently dropped to the sand.

"Residual magic still lives within these chains," Amitel said, kneeling beside the remnant. "I can rebind it."

Brandon nodded and pulled a dagger from his belt. He wedged it between the lid of the crate and the frame. "Good. Now get ready, because this thing will try to escape." Their eyes met. Brandon's heart thundered in his ears as the warlock rose, nodding. Magic ignited on his fingertips. "Ready?" Brandon asked.

"I pray to the goddess that I am," Amitel muttered. "Alright. Do it."

Brandon pulled at the enchantment that trapped the oracle within. The wood groaned, nails popping free, but the magic was strong. He gritted his teeth and let out a deep groan, releasing the dagger for a moment to grasp either side with his hands. The bent blade tumbled to the ground, but he didn't see it, instead meeting the frantic eye of a shrouded creature within.

"Amitel," Brandon warned. The creature moved from the shadows and entered the fracture of light; grey skin tightened over long, thick bones, a yellowed cloak draped over its twisted body. Blackened vines coiled around its ankles and wrists, up mangled shoulders and knees to wrap around its chest and torso.

It stepped towards Brandon, and he almost lost his grip on the lid. He grunted, eyes snapped shut, and with what strength he had, peeled the lid from the crate and watched it land in the sand at his feet.

The oracle stepped from the crate, eyes drawn to chains. *"You have freed me."*

"Not for long," Amitel replied. The oracle's eyes snapped up to meet his. "You will not leave this cave again."

It hissed, but Amitel lifted his hand, and the chains rose from the ground and struck the oracle, clamping around its thin ankles and throat. The creature screamed as the chains dragged it back into its alcove, away from Brandon and the crate.

Amitel danced out of its grasp and moved to Brandon's side. "Well, that was fairly easy," the warlock said, head cocked. "I guess it's time we leave. Hide this place so no one else can wander in and steal you away."

The oracle hissed again and rose. "*But you have not seen your future.*" It wiggled its long fingers in their directions. "*Don't you wish to know your fates?*"

From the corner of his eye, Brandon considered Amitel. Enya's words were like a sharp knife to his heart as he remembered her warnings of war, that perhaps he could have stopped Isolde's death had he known.

He closed his eyes, sucking in a breath.

"No," Amitel snapped. Brandon looked over and found the warlock watching him. "No."

"Enya had a point." Brandon took a step forward, cocking his head. "If I had known sooner about Isolde, I would have done more to stop her."

Amitel jumped in front of him, grabbing hold of his upper arm. "You do not need to see your fate, Brandon Thorne. It will not change the past."

Their eyes locked; Brandon's heart hammered in his chest, the warmth of the tunnel not fazing as ice froze in his veins. He knew he should listen to Amitel and heed his warnings, and yet Enya's words replayed in his mind. He wanted—*needed*—to know if he would have had a chance to change any of it.

Brandon tore his gaze from Amitel's and pulled his arm from his grasp, and stalked towards the oracle. It shifted form in front of his eyes, turning from strange creature to doe-eyed girl, innocent, vulnerable.

It didn't stop him from drawing his sword.

"What is my fate?"

It cocked its head. "*When the next Ecix rises, you will be there,*" it whispered, eyes flashing black. "*You will be there when the power is reborn, when the new one Ascends. You will both be there.*" Its gaze flashed to Amitel, who approached slowly. From the corner of his eye, Brandon noticed magic crackling at the tips of his fingers.

Brandon dragged the tip of his sword through the sand, and the creature's eyes snapped back to his. "What else?" he asked.

"*There will be a terrible darkness hunting her. It will almost take her.*" It closed its eyes and hummed.

Brandon felt Amitel at his back. "And?"

"*You are both merely pawns for a greater entity.*" Its eyes snapped open, and the shadows around them shifted.

Brandon could do nothing as the darkness took hold, and carried him into his destiny.

~

Fractured sunlight greeted them as they stumbled into the valley. Brandon crashed into a nearby pillar and sucked in a breath, his mind racing with images, a voice familiar yet strange, and a girl he once loved, reborn into another.

He shut his eyes and calmed his racing heart. The oracle had been cruel in its visions, all crashing through his mind like a tidal wave. He couldn't sort through them, couldn't make out anything important—

Cool fingers touched his temple, and the visions cleared. When he opened his eyes, he found Amitel standing over him, a strange look in his golden eyes. "They'll come back over time," he said, voice dull. "I just took away the strength of them, otherwise they'll drive you mad."

Brandon swallowed and nodded. "Thank you."

The warlock stepped back and turned towards the entrance of the cave. "We cannot let anyone else find the oracle. It knows too much."

Brandon frowned. Amitel lifted his hands and whispered a spell. The ground rumbled, and the temple entrance shuddered, a shimmering golden light glazing over the doorway. As it flickered out of sight, a small tree appeared in its place, growing to the size of the ones surrounding them in the valley.

Sucking in a breath, Brandon straightened. "What did you do?"

"I hid the doorway," Amitel replied. "The tree is an anchor for the magic. Perhaps one day you will be able to find it again. But I hope no one else will ever locate the entrance."

"What now?" Brandon stepped up to Amitel's side and watched him from the corner of his eye. "You will return to Varun, help rebuild. But I have no path, not without those visions."

Amitel released a heavy breath. "Your fate is intertwined with the Ecix." A sadness darkened his eyes, red filling the irises. "You do what you need to do in order to survive so you can be by her side."

"Survive." Brandon shook his head and closed his eyes. "I should be dead."

"But you aren't." Amitel turned to face him and offered his hand. "You survived the Brotherhood, the Blood Witches, and the Resurgence. You survived this. You will survive, because you came here to find your fate. Your fate is the Ecix. For some reason, she chose you. Time to figure out why."

Brandon clenched his jaw and took Amitel's hand. "Until next time, warlock."

He offered a smirk and pulled away. "I certainly hope not, Knight."

The valley was silent as Brandon walked away, no destination in mind. He did not know when the next Ecix would be born, when he would be needed, but he would be prepared. He would need to be stronger, better, should the darkness the oracle warned him of arise once more.

If it was hunting her like the oracle warned, then he would be ready.

He would not let her die again.

SIGN UP FOR THE MONTHLY NEWSLETTER

FOR EXCLUSIVE ACCESS TO NEW MATERIAL, SPECIAL OFFERS, DISCOUTS, SHORT STORIES, UPDATES, AND INFO ON NEW RELEASES FROM THE AUTHOR:

THE SERIES CONTINUES...

THE ASCENT OF THE ECIX

SHADOWLAND SAGA BOOK 3

ABOUT THE AUTHOR

Stephanie Anne grew up in different parts of Australia before her parents settled down in a small, beachside town in Northern New South Wales. There, she developed her love of reading and began penning The Lost Prince of Cadira.

Now, Stephanie lives on the Gold Coast with her family and two fur babies, avoiding the sun and spending her time drinking coffee, scrolling TikTok, and working on her next book.

https://www.stephanieanneauthor.com/

ACKNOWLEDGMENTS

Before anything else, I want to give a huge thanks to Lyra Parrish/The Courtney Project for her live streams that helped me write this book in a few days (the first draft anyway). I would never have finished THE LAST ORACLE OF LAZIROTH without Courtney and her sprints.

Like always, I need to thank my mother, Jenny, and little sister, Emily, for their continued support. Without it, I definitely would not be here! And Arya, you big goofball, for always coming in and giving me little kisses when I least expect it.

A huge thank you to Jenny D. and Dee who helped me come to the decision that I should write Thorne's side story as a novella. Their amazing help being alpha readers means a lot to me, and this entire series.

My betas: Jenny D., Elvira, Hope, Robin, and Jess. Thank you so much for giving this novella a chance, and for enjoying it!

Obviously, I need to give thanks to Celin, my cover designer, who jumped in when I asked for this at the last minute. Who created the absolute BEST cover for this novella.

Thank you to you, reader, for giving Thorne's story a chance! I'm definitely sure he appreciates it!

And last but not least, thank you to all the melted Christmas chocolate I ate while finishing this book. Could not have done it without you!

www.ingramcontent.com/pod-product-compliance
Lightning Source LLC
Chambersburg PA
CBHW030413120726
47904CB00007B/2263